U0088388

你一定要會的

Hi! How are you

基本問候語

你一定要會的基本問候語

Hi, how are you?

contents

contents

contents

contents

contents

ontents

contents

contents

contents

基本用語

Track 001

Hi.

嗨!

深入分析

隨口打招呼的用語，適用在要開口問候前使用，或當成有其他事要說明時的開場語，有打破沈默的意味。適用對象遍及所有人，正式與非正式場合也都適用。

應用會話

A: Hi. My name is David.
嗨!我的名字是大衛。

B: I'm Tracy.
我是崔西!

A: Good to meet you.
真高興認識你!

A: Hello, Mrs. White.
你好，懷特太太!

B: Oh, hi, David. How are you?
喔，嗨，大衛。你好嗎?

A: Good. How about you?
我很好，你好嗎?

基本用語

Track 002

Hello.

你好！

深入分析

除了是吸引對方注意聽、往你這裡看，也可以當成單獨使用的打招呼用語，表示「你好」的意思。後面也可以搭配其他的問候語，例如Good morning.或是How are you?以及Good to see you.等。

應用會話

A: Hello.
你好!

B: Hi, how are you?
嗨，你好嗎?

A: Pretty good. And you?
我很好!你呢?

A: Hello. Good morning.
你好!早安!

B: Good morning. Busy now?
早安!在忙嗎?

A: No, not at all. What's up?
不，一點都不會。有什麼事嗎?

基本用語

Track 003

Hi, there.

嗨，你好！

深入分析

這句Hi, there.和「那裡」(there)可是一點關係都沒有喔，而是非常普遍的美式用語，是口語化打招呼用語，意思也是「你好」的意思。和上一句的Hello比較起來，Hi, there.是更隨性的用法。

應用會話

A: Hi, there.
嗨，你好！

B: David? It's been a long time.
大衛?好久不見了！

A: Yeah. I can't believe it's almost two years.
是啊！不敢相信快兩年了吧！

A: Hi, there.
嗨，你好！

B: Hey, glad to see you.
嘿！很高興見到你。

A: Me, too.
我也是！

基本用語

Track 004

Hey.

嘿!

深入分析

表示要對方仔細聽好的意思，適合在打斷對方正在忙時，或原本沒注意到你時的情境下使用。

應用會話

A: Hey.
嘿!

B: David? What are you doing here?
大衛?你怎麼會在這裡?

A: I'm here to pick up my wife.
我來接我太太!

A: Hey, David.
嘿!大衛!

B: Tracy? Where have you been?
崔西，你人都去哪啦?

A: I was out of town on business matters.
我出城出差去了。

基本用語

Track 005

Hello, guys.

哈囉，各位好！

深入分析

在招呼語後面加上對方的名字會顯得更加尊重對方，但若面對的是一群人，無法一一點名時，就可以用guys表示，一般來說，guys的表示對象是一群男性，但偶爾也可以代表有男有女時的一群人。

應用會話

A: Hello, guys.
哈囉，各位好！

B: David? Is that you?
大衛，是你嗎？

C: Hi, David. It's been a long time.
大衛！好久不見了！

類似用法

☞ Hello, ladies.
哈囉，各位女士大家好！

☞ Hello, gentlemen.
哈囉，各位先生大家好！

☞ Hello, ladies and gentlemen.
哈囉，各位先生、各位女士大家好！

基本用語

Track 006

How are you?

你好嗎?

深入分析

問候的最基本用語，正式與非正式場合都適用。若要問候的對象為第三方以外的人，則改為以下說法：

How is he?（他好嗎?）

How is she?（她好嗎?）

How is David?（大衛好嗎?）

應用會話

A: How are you?
你好嗎?

B: Great, thanks.
我很好，謝謝!

A: Hello, Bob.
鮑伯，你好!

B: Hi, how are you?
嗨，你好嗎?

A: Good. Thanks for your concern.
我很好。謝謝你的關心!

基本用語

Track 007

How are you doing?

你好嗎？

深入分析

非常美式的問候語，字面意思似乎是問對方如何做的意思，但其實是打招呼，表示「你好嗎?」是非正式用語。

應用會話

A: Good morning, Paul.
保羅，早安!

B: Good morning, Kenny. How are you doing?
早安啊，肯尼。你好嗎?

A: Great.
很好啊!

A: How are you doing?
你好嗎?

B: Pretty good. And you?
我很好!你呢?

類似用法

☞ How are you?
你好嗎?

基本用語

Track 008

How is your father?

你父親好嗎?

深入分析

是問候句How are you?的衍生語句，主要是問候第三方以外的人，be動詞是使用is，後方可加任何的第三人稱，例如：he、she、your son、his uncle、人名...等。

應用會話

A: How is your father?
你父親好嗎?

B: He's good. Thanks for your concern.
他很好。謝謝你的關心!

A: Sure.
不客氣啦!

A: How is your mather?
你母親好嗎?

B: It's getting worse, I guess.
我猜越來越糟了。

基本用語

Track 009

How is Mr. White?

懷特先生好嗎?

深入分析

問候特定第三方的狀況，可以點名道姓問候，例如問候某位先生（Mr.+姓氏）、某問女士（Mrs.／Ms.+姓氏）或某職稱對象（職稱+姓氏）...等。

應用會話

A: How is Mr. White?
懷特先生好嗎?

B: All right.
還不錯!

A: How is Mrs. White?
懷特太太好嗎?

B: Not bad.
不錯啊!

A: How is Doctor White?
懷特醫師好嗎?

B: He is great.
他很好。

基本用語

Track 010

How is your family?

你的家人好嗎?

深入分析

這句的family是以一整個家族或家人為主，所以動詞仍舊是使用單數be動詞的is。

應用會話

A: How is your family?
你的家人好嗎?

B: Just fine. Thanks.
還好，謝謝。

A: How is your family?
你的家人好嗎?

B: Pretty good.
很好。

基本用語

Track 011

How do you do?

你好嗎?

深入分析

問候的最正式用語，通常是問候對話方的用語，不像前面的How are you?可以問候第三者，很少會使用像是"How does he do?"的句子。

應用會話

A: How do you do?
你好嗎?

B: Fine, thanks.
不錯，謝謝!

A: David, this is Mrs. Branson.
大衛，這位是布朗森太太。

B: How do you do, Mrs. Branson?
布朗森太太，你好嗎?

C: Nice to meet you, David.
大衛，很高興認識你!

基本用語

Track 012

How are you this morning?

今早過得好嗎?

深入分析

How are you?的衍生用法，問候對方特定時間（今天早上）的狀況。

應用會話

A: How are you this morning?
今早過得好嗎?

B: Fine, thank you. How about you?
好，謝謝。你呢?

A: How are you this morning?
今早過得好嗎?

B: Very well. How about you?
很好。你怎麼樣?

A: Terrible, I guess.
我想我糟透了!

類似用法

☞ How are you this evening?
今晚過得好嗎?

☞ How are you this afternoon?
今天下午過得好嗎?

基本用語

Track 013

How are you today?

你今天過得好嗎?

深入分析

How are you?的衍生用法，問候對方特定時間（今天一整天）過得如何的意思。

應用會話

A: How are you today?
你今天過得好嗎?

B: Good. How are you?
我很好。你好嗎?

A: Not so good.
不太好!

A: David?
大衛?

B: Hey! How are you today?
嘿!你今天過得好嗎?

A: Fine, just fine. And you?
好，很好。你呢?

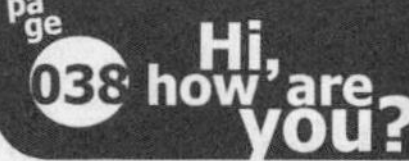

基本用語

Track 014

How are things going with you?

你現在好嗎?

深入分析

表示可能熟悉對方的某些事件，例如考試、求職、身體狀況...等，所以問候一下事情的發展狀況。

應用會話

A: How are things going with you?
你現在好嗎?

B: I feel much better now. Thank you.
我現在覺得好多了，謝謝!

A: By the way, how are things going with you?
順便問一下，你現在好嗎?

B: Like always, I'm very busy.
就像平常一樣，我總是很忙!

基本用語

Track 015

How are things?

事情都順利吧?

深入分析

不管是人事物，只要和對話方有關的事，都可以一併問候、關心，所以是使用things的複數用法。

應用會話

A: Hello. How are things?
嗨!事情都順利吧?

B: Fine, thank you. How are you?
很好，謝謝你。你好嗎?

A: How are things?
事情都順利吧?

B: Just OK. And you?
過得去!你呢?

A: Still the same.
還是老樣子啊!

類似用法

☞ How is everything?
事情都順利吧?

☞ Is everything all right?
凡事都好吧?

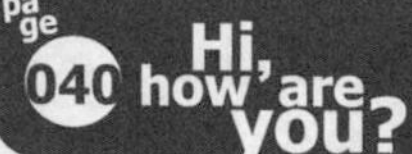

基本用語

Track 016

How did it go?

事情順利吧?

深入分析

表示雙方都知道正在進行的某件事，詢問目前進行到何種程度、發展的狀況如何的意思。

應用會話

A: How did it go, Jane?
珍，事情順利吧?

B: Everything went well.
一切都順利。

A: How did it go?
事情順利吧?

B: Terrible. I didn't finish my report last week.
糟透了!我上星期沒有完成我的報告。

基本用語

Track 017

How have you been?

近來好嗎?

深入分析

表示好一陣子沒有和對方見面了，所以通常是使用完成句，以問候一下這段時間以來對方的狀況如何的意思。

應用會話

A: How have you been?
近來好嗎?

B: Pretty good.
很好。

A: You look a bit tired.
你看起來有點累。

B: I'm OK. Don't worry.
我很好啊!別擔心!

類似用法

☞ How are you getting on?
你怎麼樣?

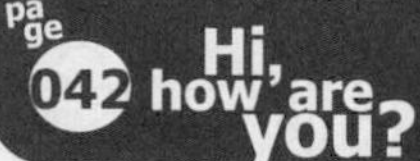

基本用語

Track 018

How's it been going?

近來如何?

深入分析

表示最近這一段時間以來，和對方相關的事件的發展狀況，所以也是用完成式(How has...)的問候語句。

應用會話

A: Buddy, how's it been going?
兄弟，近來好嗎?

B: Not very well.
不太順利!

A: What happened?
怎麼啦?

A: How's it been going, Kenny?
肯尼，近來好嗎?

B: I got divorced last month.
我上個月離婚了。

A: I'm sorry to hear that.
真是遺憾!

基本用語

Track 019

What's new?

近來好嗎?

深入分析

想知道最近對方有沒有發生什麼你不知道的事，適用好一陣子沒見面的朋友，也是代表你亟欲知道對方是否有什麼新鮮事可以和你分享。

應用會話

A: What's new?
近來好嗎?

B: Nothing much.
沒什麼事!

類似用法

☞ Anything new?
近來如何?

☞ What's up?
近來如何?

基本用語

Track 020

How was your day at work?

今天工作順利嗎?

深入分析

表示問候對方今天的工作狀況是否順利的意思，at work就是在工作時的意思。

應用會話

A: How was your day at work?
今天工作順利嗎?

B: I was fired.
我被炒魷魚了!

A: How was your day at work?
今天工作順利嗎?

B: I didn't go to work.
我沒有去上班。

A: Why not? What happened?
為什麼沒有? 發生什麼事了?

基本用語

Track 021

What happened?

發生什麼事了?

深入分析

當有意外發生，可以說"What happened?"表示希望能夠有人能夠告知事情的來龍去脈。

應用會話

A: What happened?
發生什麼事了?

B: David broke up with Cathy.
大衛和凱西分手了!

A: You look upset. What happened?
你看起來很憂愁。發生什麼事?

B: Nothing at all!
沒事啊!

類似用法

☞ What's happening?
發生什麼事?

☞ What's going on?
發生什麼事了?

基本用語

Track 022

What's the matter?

有問題嗎?

深入分析

matter是事件的意思，在這裡表示發生何事的關心用語。

應用會話

A: What's the matter?
有問題嗎?

B: I lost my keys.
我弄丟我的鑰匙了!

A: Can't you see that?
你沒看見嗎?

B: Nope. What's the matter?
沒有啊!有問題嗎?

類似用法

☞ What's the matter here?
這裡發生什麼事了?

基本用語

Track 023

What's the matter with you?

你發生什麼事了?

深入分析

當明顯發現對方不太對勁時，就可以直接開門見山，關心對方發生什麼事了!

應用會話

A: What's the matter with you?
你發生什麼事了?

B: I think I failed my math test.
我想我考砸了數學考試。

A: I feel awful.
我覺得糟透了!

B: What's the matter with you?
你發生什麼事了?

類似用法

☞ What happened to you?
你發生什麼事了?

基本用語

Track 024

What's the problem?

有什麼問題嗎?

深入分析

當問題發生時，你想要知道問題(problem)的癥結點或發生的原因時，就可以問"What's the problem?"

應用會話

A: What's the problem, David?
大衛，有什麼問題嗎?

B: I'm really in a bad mood today.
我今天的心情不好!

A: You look pale. What's the problem?
你看起來好蒼白!有什麼問題嗎?

B: I don't feel well.
我覺得不舒服。

類似用法

☞ What's wrong?
有問題嗎?

基本用語

Track 025

What's your problem?

你腦袋有問題嗎?

深入分析

字面意思雖然是「你的問題是什麼」，但若用責難的語氣，則可以表示「問題出在你」，類似中文「你的頭殼壞了嗎?」的質疑。

應用會話

A: What's your problem?
你腦袋有問題嗎?

B: Pardon?
你說什麼啊?

A: Oh, shit! What's your problem?
喔，糟糕。你腦袋有問題嗎?

B: Not me!
不是我啦!

基本用語

Track 026

What's the trouble?

怎麼了？

深入分析

表示想要知道是什麼原因造成對方的困擾。trouble是麻煩事的意思。

應用會話

A: What's the trouble?
怎麼了？

B: I think I failed my math test.
我想我搞砸了我的數學考試。

A: What's the trouble?
怎麼了？

B: I shouldn't have gone to see a movie last week.
我上星期不應該去看電影。

基本用語

Track 027

Is there something wrong?

有什麼問題嗎?

深入分析

表示某事(something)發生，且是你我可能都知道這件事，且事件不太尋常的意思。

應用會話

A: Is there something wrong?
有什麼問題嗎?

B: My leg hurts.
我的腳好痛喔!

A: Is there something wrong? You look upset.
有什麼問題嗎?你看起來很沮喪。

B: Nothing. I just feel sick.
沒事，我只是覺得不舒服。

類似用法

☞ Something wrong?
有什麼問題嗎?

基本用語

Track 028

Is that a problem?

有困難嗎?

深入分析

當你做出結論或下決定後，就可以徵詢在場的所有人"Is that a problem?"，表示若有問題，請趕緊提出來的意思。

應用會話

A: Is that a problem?
有困難嗎?

B: Nothing. I can handle it by myself.
沒事!我可以自己處理!

A: OK! That's all for now.
好了!現在就這樣!

B: Mr. White!
懷特先生!

A: Yes? Is that a problem?
請說!有困難嗎?

基本用語

Track 029

What's up?

有事嗎?

深入分析

當對方有所求時，你就可以表明"What's up?"，表示「有什麼事趕緊說吧!」的意思。

應用會話

A: Hey, Kenny, got a minute?
嘿，肯尼，有空嗎?

B: Sure. What's up?
當然。有事嗎?

A: Can I talk to you for a moment?
我能和你說說話嗎?

B: Sure. What's up?
當然可以。有什麼事嗎?

類似用法

☞ What's wrong?
怎麼啦?

基本用語

Track 030

Yes?

怎麼啦?

深入分析

yes可以是「答應」、「是的」的意思，但這裡使用疑問語氣，則是表示「什麼事?你趕緊說」，是鼓勵對方繼續說明的意思。

應用會話

A: David? Got a minute?
大衛，有空嗎?

B: Yes?
怎麼啦?

A: I have a question.
我有一個問題要問。

A: Mr. Jones! I... well... I wanna...
瓊斯先生!我...嗯...我想要...

B: Yes? Still have questions?
怎麼啦?還有問題嗎?

A: No, no, no, not at all.
沒啦!沒有啊!

基本用語

Track 031

I'm doing great.

我過得不錯。

深入分析

針對對方隨口的問候，一般來說，可以制式化地說"I'm fine."，但另一種常見的回答則是"I'm doing great."，可以顯得英文不會那麼老套！

應用會話

A: Hi, David. How are you?
嗨，大衛。你好嗎?

B: I'm doing great.
我過得不錯。

A: I'm doing great.
我過得不錯。

B: Good for you.
很好。

類似用法

☞ I'm fine.
不錯啊!

☞ Good.
很好啊!

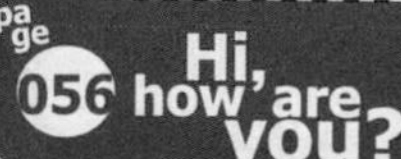

基本用語

Track 032

I'm OK.

我很好!

深入分析

當對方關心你是否感到不適時，你要表明自己很好、沒有問題時，就可以說"I'm OK."，也可以表示「我可以自己處理」的意思。

應用會話

A: Let me drive you to the hospital.
我開車送你去醫院。

B: Don't worry about it. I'm OK.
不用擔心!我很好!

A: No. You are not. Come on.
不，你一點都不好吧!走吧!

A: Let me help you with those bags.
讓我幫你拿這些袋子。

B: I'm OK.
我可以自己處理!

類似用法

☞ I'm all right.
我沒事的!

基本用語

Track 033

Where are you off to?

你要去哪裡?

深入分析

當你出門在外遇到熟人時，就可以順口問對方"Where are you off to?"表示關心對方要去何處的意思。

應用會話

A: Where are you guys off to?
你們一群人要去哪裡?

B: We are going to see a movie.
我們要去看電影。

C: Would you like to join us?
你要和我們一起去嗎?

A: Yes, I'd love to.
好啊!我很樂意去。

類似用法

☞ Where are you going?
你要去哪裡?

☞ Where are you headed?
你要去哪裡?

基本用語

Track 034

So?

所以呢?

深入分析

當對方發表言論而你有質疑時，就可以用疑問的語氣說"So?"，意思是「那又如何?」或是「所以說呢?」，表示希望對方能夠再多加解釋的意思。

應用會話

A: David is off today.
大衛今天沒來上班。

B: So?
所以呢?

A: Maybe you should let Carol know right now.
也許你現在應該要讓凱蘿知道一下!

A: Is that all?
就這樣嗎?

B: So?
所以呢?

A: Is there anything else to discuss?
還有沒有什麼要討論的?

基本用語

Track 035

Same as always.

老樣子!

深入分析

回應對方的關心，表示對方自己還是「老樣子」時，就可以說: "Same as always."。

應用會話

A: How are you doing?
近來好嗎?

B: You know, same as always.
你知道的，老樣子!

A: How are things going?
事情進展得怎樣?

B: Well, same as always.
嗯，老樣子囉!

類似用法

☞ The same as usual!
一如往常!

☞ Still the same.
老樣子。

基本用語

Track 036

Not as good as usual.

不像平常那麼好!

深入分析

面對他人的關心問候，你可以坦白表示不像以前那麼好:"Not as good as usual."但回答這句話的前提是，對方和你必須有一定的交情，也知道你平常的狀況，否則誰會知道你平常(usual)的狀況呢?

應用會話

A: How are things going?
事情進展得怎樣?

B: Not as good as usual.
不像平常那麼好!

A: That's too bad.
真是糟糕!

A: How is my work?
我的工作表現如何?

B: Not as good as usual.
不像平常那麼好!

基本用語

Track 037

Not so good.

沒有那麼好！

深入分析

當對方問候你，除了制式回答"Fine."之外，你也可以照實回答「實際的狀況沒有想像中好」，英文就叫做"Not so good."。

應用會話

A: How is business?
生意如何?

B: Not so good.
沒有那麼好!

A: How do you feel now?
你現在覺得如何?

B: Not so good.
沒有那麼好!

基本用語

Track 038

Not as good as I thought.

沒有像我自己想像中的這麼好！

深入分析

若是你的狀況不如你自己之前想像中或預期的好，就可以說"Not as good as I thought."。

應用會話

A: How is everything?
你好嗎？

B: Not as good as I thought.
沒有像我自己想像中的這麼好！

A: How come?
怎麼會這樣呢？

B: Who knows?
誰知道？

基本用語

Track 039

Nothing special.

沒什麼特別的事！

深入分析

當對方問候有沒有什麼新鮮事可以分享時，中文可以回答「沒什麼特別的事」，英文就可以說"Nothing special."表示一切如常的意思。也可以適用在回答對方「沒有什麼特別發現」的情境。

應用會話

A: What's new?
近來好嗎?

B: Nothing special.
沒什麼特別的事!

A: Do you have any idea?
有什麼主意嗎?

B: Nothing special.
沒什麼特別的!

A: How was the movie?
電影好看嗎?

B: Nothing special.
沒什麼特別的!

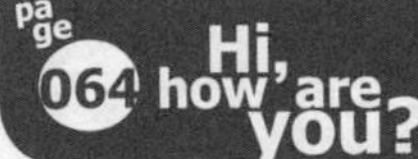

基本用語

Track 040

So far so good.

都還過得去!

深入分析

若是你的狀況截至目前為止都還不錯、馬馬虎虎的，中文是「都還過得去!」，英文就可以回答"So far so good."。

應用會話

A: How are you doing, pal?
你好嗎，伙伴?

B: So far so good.
都還過得去!

A: How have you been?
你過得好嗎?

B: So far so good.
都還過得去!

A: Good to hear that.
很好!

基本用語

Track 041

So-so.

馬馬虎虎啦!

深入分析

狀況普普通通，沒有大好也沒有大壞，中文就是「馬馬虎虎!」英文就是"So-so."表示「就是如此」的意思。

應用會話

A: How was the party?
派對好玩嗎?

B: So-so.
馬馬虎虎啦!

A: How is everything?
事情都還好吧?

B: So-so.
馬馬虎虎啦!

基本用語

Track 042

Not too bad.

不差!

深入分析

若你的狀況沒有很好，但也不會太差，也可以回答"Not too bad."表示「不差」，也就是「還可以過得去」的意思。

應用會話

A: How is your exam?
你考試考得如何?

B: Not too bad.
不差!

A: How is everything going?
事情都順利吧?

B: Not too bad, I guess.
我猜不太糟糕!

基本用語

Track 043

Nothing is happening.

沒事啊!

深入分析

當對方問候有沒有什麼事情發生，而你的狀況平淡如水，就可以回答"Nothing is happening."表示沒有任何狀況發生的意思。

應用會話

A: You look terrible.
你看起來很糟糕!

B: Nothing is happening.
沒事啊!

A: What's going on?
發生了什麼事?

B: Nothing is happening.
沒事啊!

A: Something wrong today?
今天有什麼問題嗎?

B: Nothing is happening today.
今天沒什麼事啊!

基本用語

Track 044

That's about it.

事情大概就是這樣!

深入分析

當你向對方詳細說明發生的事情後，就可以在結語時說"That's about it."表示「狀況就如同以上我說的，其他沒了」，有「我說完了!」的意思。

應用會話

A: See? It's so easy to handle it on your own.
看吧!自己處理很簡單吧!

B: That's all?
就這樣?

A: Yup! That's about it.
是啊!事情大概就是這樣!

B: OK. You owe me one.
好吧!你欠我一個人情。

A: That's about it.
事情大概就是這樣!

B: I don't think so.
我不這麼認為!

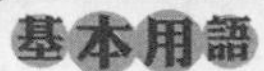

Track 045

Did you hear about what happened?

你有聽說發生什麼事了嗎?

深入分析

表示探詢對方是否知道什麼不尋常的事情發生，這裡的hear不但是「聽到...」、「聽說...」，也代表「知道...」的意思。

應用會話

A: Did you hear about what happened?
你有聽說發生什麼事了嗎?

B: Nope.
沒有啊!

A: Did you hear about what happened?
你有聽說發生什麼事了嗎?

B: Yup. David is in hospital.
有啊!大衛住院了。

基本用語

Track 046

I heard about what happened.

我有聽說發生的事了!

深入分析

表示自己已經耳聞、也知道了對方所指的事情是為何事的意思。

應用會話

A: Hey, pal, I heard about what happened.
嘿，伙伴，我有聽說發生的事了!

B: Come on, I'm pretty good.
別這樣!我蠻好的。

A: I heard about what happened.
我有聽說發生的事了!

B: You did?
是嗎?

類似用法

☞ I heard about what happened to you.
我有聽說發生在你身上的事了!

基本用語

Track 047

Good luck.

祝你好運!

深入分析

對即將要遠行者、有更遠大目標要執行，或有一段時間彼此會無法見面者的祝福，就可以說: "Good luck." 。

應用會話

A: Good luck.
祝你好運!

B: Thanks. I really need it.
謝謝，我真的需要（好運氣）。

類似用法

☞ Wish you good luck.
祝你好運。

☞ Good luck to you.
祝你好運。

☞ Good luck, kids.
孩子們，祝你們好運!

☞ Good luck to you, pal.
伙伴，祝你好運。

☞ Good luck to you and your family.
祝你和你的家人好運喔!

基本用語

Track 048

Good-bye!

再見!

深入分析

道別的最常用語，就是"Good-bye!"，不論是正式或非正式、認識或陌生人之間，都可以在分手時，來上一句:"Good-bye!"。

應用會話

A: I'll be leaving.
我要離開了。

B: Good-bye!
再見!

A: Are you taking off?
你要走了嗎?

B: Yeah. Good-bye!
是啊!再見!

A: Take care.
保重啦!

B: You too! Good-bye!
你也是!再見!

基本用語

Track 049

See you next time.

下次見。

深入分析

道別時除了說:"Good-bye!"之外，還可以補上一句:"See you next time."，表示期待再見面的意思。

應用會話

A: Wow, it's pretty late now.
哇!現在很晚了。

B: OK, that's it. See you next time.
是啊，就這樣。下次見囉!

A: Here comes my bus. See you next time.
我的公車來了。下次見囉!

B: Bye!
再見!

類似用法

☞ See you.
再見!

☞ See you around.
再見!

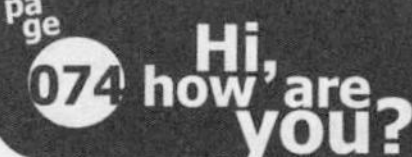

基本用語

Track 050

See you in a few minutes.

等會見!

深入分析

通常適用在稍後可能還會再見面的情境，例如你只是要出門去買杯咖啡時，就可以告訴同事:"See you in a few minutes."，表示「馬上回來」、「等會就可以再見面」的意思。

應用會話

A: See you in a few minutes.
等會見!

B: Fine. I'll be expecting you.
好的。我會等你喔!

A: Nice meeting you.
很高興認識你!

B: You too. See you in a few minutes.
我也是。等會見!

類似用法

☞ See you later.
再見!

基本用語

Track 051

I'd like to introduce Bob.

我來介紹一下鮑伯。

深入分析

"I'd like to introduce + someone"，表示在正式場合，要將某人介紹給大家認識的用語。

應用會話

A: I'd like to introduce Bob.
我來介紹一下鮑伯。

B: Nice to meet you, Bob.
鮑伯，很高興認識你。

C: Nice to see you, too.
（我也）很高興認識你。

類似用法

☞ Allow me to introduce Miss Smith.
請允許由我來介紹史密斯小姐。

基本用語

Track 052

Bob, let me introduce Mr. Jones.

鮑伯，我來介紹一下瓊斯先生。

深入分析

特地告知某人要介紹第三者給他認識的用語，所以會在句子前面先稱呼對方，再介紹第三方的名字或身份。

應用會話

A: Bob, let me introduce Mr. Jones.
鮑伯，我來介紹一下瓊斯先生。

B: I'm glad to meet you, Mr. Jones.
瓊斯先生，我很高興認識你。

C: My pleasure to meet you.
能認識你是我的榮幸。

類似用法

☞ Let me introduce my friend Bob to you.
讓我把我的朋友鮑伯介紹給你。

☞ Allow me to introduce you to Mr. Baker.
請允許由我把你介紹給貝克先生。

基本用語

Track 053

I'd like you to meet Bob.

我想讓你來見一下鮑伯。

深入分析

meet是見面的意思，在介紹的場合，則有彼此見面認識的意思，正式或非正式場合皆適用。

應用會話

A: Tracy, I'd like you to meet Bob.
崔西，我想讓你來見一下鮑伯。

B: Nice to meet you, Bob.
鮑伯，很高興認識你。

C: Nice to meet you, too, Tracy.
崔西，我也很高興認識妳。

A: I'd like you to meet Bob.
我想讓你來見一下鮑伯。

B: Hi, Bob!
鮑伯，你好！

C: You must be Tracy.
你一定是崔西！

基本用語

Track 054

Come to see my friend.

來認識一下我的朋友!

深入分析

和meet類似，see是見面的意思，這句也有認識新朋友的意思，屬於非正式場合使用。

應用會話

A: Come to see my friend.
來認識一下我的朋友!

B: Not now, please. I'm exhausted.
拜託不要現在!我累壞了!

A: Come to see my roommate. Chris, this is Jane.
來認識一下我的室友。克里斯，這是珍。

B: Nice to meet you, Chris.
克里斯，很高興認識你。

C: Nice to meet you, too.
我也很高興認識你。

基本用語

Track 055

This is Chris.

這位是克里斯。

深入分析

要說明被介紹者的名字或身份時，就可以使用"this is + 名字／身份"的句型。

應用會話

A: This is Chris. And this is Tracy.
這位是克里斯。而這位是崔西。

B: I've heard so much about you.
久仰大名!

C: Nothing bad, I hope.
希望都不是壞事!

A: Jane, this is Chris. Chris, this is Jane, my sister.
珍，這是克里斯。克里斯，這是我妹妹珍。

B: How do you do, Chris?
克里斯，你好嗎?

C: Fine.
我很好!

基本用語

Track 056

I'm pleased to meet you.

我很高興認識你。

深入分析

認識新朋友時，一定來句客套用語，這句"I'm pleased to meet you."就是非常實用的一句回應用語。

應用會話

A: My name is Tracy.
我的名字是崔西。

B: I'm pleased to meet you.
我很高興認識你。

A: We haven't met, have we? I'm Jane.
我們沒見過面，是吧? 我是珍妮。

B: I'm David. I'm pleased to meet you, Jane.
我是大衛，珍妮，很高興認識你。

類似用法

☞ It's my pleasure to meet you.
能認識你是我的榮幸。

基本用語

Track 057

Nice to meet you.

很高興能認識你。

深入分析

認識新朋友時的客套用語，全文是"It's nice to meet you."，meet雖是見面，但在這句是「認識」的意思。

應用會話

A: This is my wife Ruby. Ruby, this is David.
這是我太太，露比。露比，這是大衛。

B: Nice to meet you, Ruby.
很高興能認識你，露比。

C: Nice to meet you, too.
我也很高興認識你。

類似用法

☞ It's nice to meet you.
很高興認識你。

☞ Glad to meet you.
很高興能認識你。

☞ My pleasure to meet you.
很高興認識你!

基本用語

Track 058

I've heard a lot about you.

久仰大名!

深入分析

當你認識一位耳聞已久的新朋友時，就可以客套的回應:"I've heard a lot about you."，也就是中文「久仰大名」的意思。

應用會話

A: You must be Jane. I'm David.
你一定是珍妮，我是大衛。

B: Hi, David. I've heard a lot about you.
嗨，大衛。久仰大名!

A: It's nice to meet you. I'm Jane.
很高興認識你，我是珍妮。

B: Hi, I've heard a lot about you.
嗨，久仰大名!

類似用法

☞ I've heard so much about you.
久仰大名!

基本用語

Track 059

Are you familiar with David?

你和大衛熟嗎?

深入分析

"be familiar with someone"，表示「認識某人」的意思，可能是因為認識而瞭解，也可以是久仰大名而熟悉對方的意思。

應用會話

A: Are you familiar with David?
你和大衛熟嗎?

B: Yes. He is my uncle.
熟啊!他是我叔叔。

A: Are you familiar with David?
你和大衛熟嗎?

B: David who?
哪一位大衛?

A: David Jones.
大衛・瓊斯。

B: No, I am not. Why?
不，我不熟。為什麼要這麼問?

基本用語

Track 060

I don't think you've met Peggy.

我想你沒見過佩姬吧!

深入分析

"heve／has met someone"雖是表示已經認識某人的意思，但因為句子前面有"I don't think..."所以是否定式語句，表示一定不認識某人的意思，是引薦雙方認識前的開場用語。

應用會話

A: I don't think you've met Peggy.
我想你沒見過佩姬吧!

B: Nice to meet you, Peggy.
很高興認識妳，佩姬。

C: Nice to meet you, too, Lucy.
也很高興認識你，露西。

A: I don't think you've met Peggy.
我想你沒見過佩姬吧!

B: Peggy White? She is my sister.
佩姬．懷特? 她是我姊姊啊!

基本用語

Track 061

Have we ever met before?

我們以前見過面嗎?

深入分析

當你認識某人，或是你似乎是和對方見過面，就可以試探性地詢問:"Have we ever met before?"，也可以是想要認識新朋友的搭訕用語。

應用會話

A: You look familiar.
你看起很面熟!

B: Have we ever met before?
我們以前見過面嗎?

A: Have we ever met before?
我們以前見過面嗎?

B: I don't think so.
我不這麼認為。

A: I am David.
我是大衛。

B: I am Tracy.
我是崔西。

基本用語

Track 062

My name is Bob.

我的名字叫鮑伯。

深入分析

自我介紹的最常用句型就是"My name is + 名字"，不論是正式或非正式場合都適用。

應用會話

A: Hello, my name is Bob.
你好，我的名字叫鮑伯。

B: Hi, I'm Susan.
你好，我是蘇珊。

A: Where are you from?
你從哪兒來?

B: I'm from Taiwan.
我來自台灣。

類似用法

☞ I am Helen.
我是海倫。

基本用語

Track 063

Come on in and sit down, please.

請進來坐吧！

深入分析

當有人來拜訪你時，可別讓對方站在門外，那是不禮貌的，應請對方趕緊進來坐下，表示雙方可以好好聊聊的意思。

應用會話

A: Did I bother you?
我有打擾到你嗎？

B: No, not at all. Come on in and sit down, please.
不，一點都不會。請進來坐吧！

A: Come on in and sit down, please. Water or tea?
請進來坐吧！要喝水還是茶？

B: No, thanks.
不，不用了，謝謝！

類似用法

☞ Have a seat.
請坐！

基本用語

Track 064

Coffee?

要喝咖啡嗎?

深入分析

簡單的用飲料的名稱加上疑問句的語氣，就可以表示向對方詢問是否要喝這種飲料的意思。

應用會話

A: Coffee?
要喝咖啡嗎?

B: Yes, please.
好的，謝謝!

A: Coffee?
要喝咖啡嗎?

B: No, thanks.
不，不用了!

類似用法

☞ Would you like some coffee?
要不要喝咖啡?

☞ How about some coffee?
要不要喝咖啡?

基本用語

Track 065

Do you live around here?

你住在附近嗎?

深入分析

"around here"表示地點就在附近，是非常常見的片語句型。

應用會話

A: Do you live around here?
你住在附近嗎?

B: No, I don't.
不是。

A: Do you live around here?
你住在附近嗎?

B: Well, I'm just visiting.
這個嘛，我只是來拜訪。

基本用語

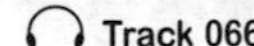

Are you OK?
你還好吧?

深入分析

當你發現對方不對勁或是臉色看起來很差時，你想要知道對方現在是否沒問題時，就可以問:"Are you OK?"。

應用會話

A: Are you OK?
你還好吧?

B: I've got a stomachache.
我的胃好痛!

A: Are you OK? You look very tired.
你還好吧? 你看起來很累耶!

B: I'm OK, except that I've got a bad cough.
還好，只是一直咳嗽。

基本用語

Track 067

How are you feeling now?

你現在感覺如何?

深入分析

當你知道對方先前身體不適，再遇到對方時，就可以問問:"How are you feeling now?"，以關心一下對方現在的狀況。

應用會話

A: How are you feeling now?
你現在感覺如何?

B: Much better now.
現在好多了!

A: How are you feeling now?
你現在感覺如何?

B: Not so good.
不太好!

A: You should see a doctor.
你應該要去看醫生。

基本用語

Track 068

I have a cold.

我感冒了！

深入分析

cold是寒冷的意思，所以「感染感冒」的說法是"have a cold"，是最普遍的口語化語句。

應用會話

A: Are you all right?
你還好吧?

B: Not too well. I have a cold.
不太好。我感冒了！

A: How are you doing?
你好嗎?

B: Terrible. I have a cold.
不太好！我感冒了！

類似用法

☞ I have caught a cold.
我感冒了！

基本用語

Track 069

I've got a fever.

我發燒了！

深入分析

fever是發熱的意思，所以發燒的用法是"get a fever"。
"have got a fever"是完成式用法，表示已經得到感冒了。

應用會話

A: You look rather pale today.
你今天臉色很蒼白。

B: I've got a fever.
我發燒了！

A: I've got a fever.
我發燒了！

B: Did you go to see a doctor?
你有去看醫生了嗎？

類似用法

☞ I've got a temperature.
我發燒了！

基本用語

Track 070

I've got a headache.

我的頭好痛!

深入分析

headache可以拆字解讀為「頭的疼痛」，也就是頭痛的意思，常見的說法為"have／get a headache"。

應用會話

A: Are you OK?
你沒事吧?

B: I've got a headache.
我的頭好痛!

A. Are you all right?
你還好吧?

B: I've got a headache.
我的頭好痛!

類似用法

☞ I've got a stomachache.
我胃痛。

基本用語

Track 071

I ache all over.

我渾身都在痛!

深入分析

"all over"表示全身上下，"ache all over"也就是全身都不舒服、疼痛的意思。

應用會話

A: What's the matter with you?
你怎麼了?

B: I ache all over.
我渾身都在痛!

A: Did you go to see a doctor?
你有去看醫生嗎?

A: You look awful.
你看起來糟透了!

B: I ache all over.
我渾身都在痛!

A: You'd better stay in bed.
你最好躺在床上休息。

基本用語

Track 072

I can't eat.

我無法進食!

深入分析

字面意思是無法吃，也就是無法進食、食不下嚥的意思，造成的原因可能是因為生理的不適或心理因素。

應用會話

A: How have you been?
近來好嗎?

B: I can't eat.
我無法進食!

A: Let me drive you to see a doctor.
我開車送你去看醫生吧!

A: How are you feeling now?
你現在感覺如何?

B: I can't eat.
我無法進食!

基本用語

Track 073

I can't stop coughing.

我不停地咳嗽。

深入分析

"stop + 動名詞"，表示「停不住做某事」的意思，也就是不由自主一直做某事或出現某種行為的意思。

應用會話

A: I can't stop coughing.
我不停地咳嗽。

B: You need to see a doctor right away.
你應該要馬上去看醫生。

A: I can't stop coughing.
我不停地咳嗽。

B: Let me take you to the hospital.
我帶你去醫院吧!

類似用法

☞ I can't stop sneezing.
我不停地打噴嚏。

基本用語

Track 074

I'm staying home from work.

我正休假在家。

深入分析

"stay home"就是字面意思待在家裡，後面再註明"from work"也就是休假在家沒有上班的意思。

應用會話

A: What's matter with you?
你怎麼啦?

B: I broke my leg.
我的腿骨骨折了!

A: Did you go to see a doctor?
你有去看醫生嗎?

B: Yes, I did. I'm staying home from work.
有啊!我正休假在家。

基本用語

Track 075

It's a bad cold.

是重感冒。

深入分析

說明是得到感冒，就說"It's a cold."，若是重感冒，則加上bad(嚴重的)說明即可。

應用會話

A: What did the doctor say?
醫生說什麼?

B: It's a bad cold.
是重感冒。

A: Can I get you something?
要我幫你買什麼嗎?

B: No, thanks.
不用了!

類似用法

☞ I've got a sore throat.
我喉嚨痛。

☞ I've got a runny nose.
我流鼻水。

☞ I've got a bad cough.
我咳嗽得厲害。

基本用語

Track 076

You should listen to the doctor.

你應該要聽醫生的話!

深入分析

"should listen to someone"表示聽從某人的話，可能是意見、指示等。

應用會話

A: What did the doctor say?
醫生說什麼?

B: My doctor told me not to drink alcohol for 2 months.
我的醫生要我兩個月不能喝酒!

A: You should listen to the doctor.
你真的應該要聽醫生的話!

A: I feel terrible.
我覺得糟透了!

B: You know what? You should listen to the doctor.
你知道嗎? 你應該要聽醫生的話!

基本用語

Track 077

You'd better stay in bed.

你最好是躺在床上休息。

深入分析

"You'd better..."全文是"You had better..."表示「你應該...」，後面接原形動詞。"stay in bed"是待在床上，也就是臥床休息的意思。

應用會話

A: I feel sick.
我覺得不舒服。

B: You'd better stay in bed.
你最好是臥床休息。

A: You'd better stay in bed.
你最好是臥床休息。

B: But I have to meet Tracy at the airport.
可是我要去機場接崔西的飛機。

基本用語

Track 078

You should get some more rest.

你要多多休息!

深入分析

對方看起來很累或不太舒服時，你就建議對方休息(get some rest)，若是中文的「多多休息」，則是"get some more rest."。

應用會話

A: I don't feel well.
我不舒服。

B: You should get some more rest.
你要多多休息!

A: I'm afraid I'll let you down.
我恐怕要讓你失望了。

B: Come on! You should get some more rest.
別這樣!你要多多休息!

基本用語

Track 079

Did you take medicine?

你有吃藥了嗎?

深入分析

當對方不舒服去看醫生，卻還是狀況不好時，你就可以關心對方是否有按時服藥:"Did you take medicine?"。吃藥的動詞是take，而不是eat。

應用會話

A: Did you take medicine?
你有吃藥了嗎?

B: Yes.
有!

A: Good. Get some sleep.
很好!先睡一下吧!

A: Did you take medicine?
你有吃藥了嗎?

B: No! But I'm fine. Don't worry!
沒有!但我很好啦!別擔心!

基本用語

Track 080

I lost it somewhere in the house.

我把它弄丟在房子裡的某個地方了！

深入分析

"lost something"表示把某物搞丟了的意思。lost是lose的過去式，這類丟掉物品的句子，時態通常為過去式。"somewhere in the house"表示在房子裡的某個地方。

應用會話

A: What are you looking for?
你在找什麼東西?

B: I lost my keys somewhere in the house.
我把鑰匙弄丟在房子裡的某個地方了！

A: I lost your magazine somewhere in the house.
我把你的雜誌弄丟在房子裡的某個地方了！

B: Never mind. It was a back issue anyway.
沒關係！反正是本過期雜誌。

基本用語

Track 081

What a surprise!

好訝異呀!

深入分析

當令人訝異的事件發生時,你就可以摀著嘴、摸著胸口,誇張的說:"What a surprise!",表示不敢相信的意思。

應用會話

A: Jack? What a surprise!
傑克? 好訝異呀!

B: Hi, Tracy. How are you doing?
嗨,崔西,你好嗎?

A: Good. How about you?
很好。你呢?

A: I can't believe it.
我真的是不敢相信!

B: Yeah! What a surprise!
是啊!好訝異呀!

基本用語

Track 082

What a coincidence!

多巧啊!

深入分析

世界是很小的，當你在路上偶遇多年不見的朋友、發生某些巧合的事時，都可以說:"What a coincidence!"。

應用會話

A: Hi, David, How are you?
嗨!大衛，你好嗎?

B: John! What a coincidence!
約翰!多巧啊!

A: Yeah. This is a small world.
是啊!世界真是小!

A: Is that Tom?
那是湯姆嗎?

B: That's right!
沒錯!

A: What a coincidence!
多巧啊!

基本用語

Track 083

Good to see you again.

真高興又見到你！

深入分析

表示和久未見面的人再次見面時的客套語。全文是"It's good to see you again."。

應用會話

A: Hi, long time no see.
嗨，好久不見了。

B: Good to see you again.
真高興又見到你！

A: You look great.
你看起來氣色真好。

A: Good to see you again.
真高興又見到你！

B: How have you been?
你好嗎？

A: Just fine. And you?
還不錯！你呢？

類似用法

☞ It's nice seeing you again.
見到你真好。

基本用語

Track 084

I haven't seen you for ages.

真是好久不見了!

深入分析

"haven't seen someone for + 時間"，表示這一段時間未曾和某人見面，也就是「好久不見」的意思。

應用會話

A: How are you?
你好嗎?

B: Hi, Linda. I haven't seen you for ages.
嗨，琳達!真是好久不見了!

A: I haven't seen you for ages.
真是好久不見了!

B: When did we meet last time?
我們上次見面是什麼時候?

類似用法

☞ I haven't seen you for a long time.
有好久沒見到你了!

☞ I haven't seen you for months.
好幾個月沒見到你了!

基本用語

Track 085

It's been a long time.

好久不見了!

深入分析

遇到久未見面的熟人時，也可以直接說:"It's been a long time."，字面意思是「真的是好久了!」，也可以表示「很久沒面見」的意思。

應用會話

A: Where have you been?
你都到哪兒去了?

B: John? I can't believe it. It's been a long time.
約翰? 不敢相信! 好久不見了!

A: Jenny, is that you?
珍妮，是你嗎?

B: Hi, David. It's me. It's been a long time.
嗨，大衛!就是我!真的是好久不見了!

基本用語

Track 086

That seems like such a long time.

好像好久喔！

深入分析

a long time是很長一段時間的意思，seem則是好像、似乎，表示時間似乎在不知不覺中就過去了！

應用會話

A: That seems like such a long time.
好像好久喔！

B: Yes, it is. It's a slow process.
是啊！這個過程是很慢的！

A: I can't wait to see her.
我迫不及待要和她見面。

A: When can he go home?
他什麼時候能回家？

B: Maybe in two days.
可能就這兩天。

A: That seems like such a long time.
好像好久喔！

基本用語

Track 087

You look great.

你看起來氣色不錯耶!

深入分析

當某人神清氣爽時，你就可以說:"You look great."，可以表示誇讚，也就是氣色看起來不錯的意思。

應用會話

A: Hi, long time no see.
嗨，好久不見了!

B: Yeah! Hey, you look great.
是啊!嘿，你看起來氣色不錯耶!

A: You look great.
你看起來氣色不錯耶!

B: You know what? I've been working out twice a day.
你知道嗎?我一直以來都一天健身兩次。

類似用法

☞ You look beautiful.
你看起來很漂亮。

☞ You look smart.
你看起來很有精神。

基本用語

Track 088

You look upset.

你看起來很沮喪喔!

深入分析

"someone look+形容詞"，表示「某人看起來...」的意思。

應用會話

A: You look upset.
你看起來很沮喪喔!

B: I'm OK.
我很好!

A: You look upset.
你看起來很沮喪喔!

B: Don't worry about me.
別擔心我!

類似用法

☞ You look pale.
你看起來臉色蒼白!

☞ You look terrible.
你看起來糟透了!

☞ You look sexy.
你看起來很性感!

基本用語

Track 089

You look tired.

你看起來累了!

深入分析

當對方的行為舉止就外貌上看起來很疲勞時，你就可以說: "You look tired."

應用會話

A: You look tired.
你看起來累了!

B: It's nothing. I was up late last night.
沒事，我昨晚太晚睡了。

A: You look tired.
你看起來累了!

B: Oh, really? I felt just fine.
真的嗎? 我還好啊!

類似用法

☞ You look a bit tired.
你看起來有點累了!

☞ You look exhausted.
你看起來很累!

基本用語

Track 090

You look familiar.

你看起來很眼熟!

深入分析

someone look familiar表示某人看起來熟悉，也就是「看起來很眼熟、我可能認識」的意思，是和可能熟識者的搭訕用語。

應用會話

A: You look familiar.
你看起來很眼熟!

B: My name is Judy.
我的名字是茱蒂。

A: Judy Black! It's nice to meet you.
你是茱蒂・布萊克!很高興認識你。

A: Haven't we met before?
我們以前沒有見過面嗎?

B: You look familiar.
你看起來很眼熟!

A: You work for HOLA, don't you?
你在HOLA工作，對吧?

基本用語

Track 091

You look worried about something.

你看起來好像在擔心什麼事。

深入分析

對方看起還憂心忡忡或心事重重時，表示擔心(worry)某事，你就可以關心地說:"You look worried about something."，something表示一些你所不知道的事。

應用會話

A: You look worried about something.
你看起來好像在擔心什麼事。

B: I'm terribly sorry, John.
真是非常抱歉，約翰。

A: What? What's the matter with you?
怎麼啦? 你發生什麼事?

A: You look worried about something.
你看起來好像在擔心什麼事。

B: Yeah! I didn't get that job.
是啊!我沒有得到那份工作。

基本用語

Track 092

Do I know you?

我們認識嗎?

深入分析

當某人和你說話時，若你不太確定自己和對方是否熟識，就可以直接回應:"Do I know you?"，可以表示「我不認識你」。若用生氣的語氣說這句話，則也可以表示「你不是個重要人物、廢話少說、我不想聽」的意思。

應用會話

A: Say, aren't you David?
嘿，你是大衛嗎?

B: Yes. Do I know you?
是的，我們認識嗎?

A: Do I know you?
我們認識嗎?

B: I think I've seen you before.
我想我以前曾見過你。

類似用法

☞ Have we met?
我們認識嗎?

基本用語

Track 093

We've known each other for a long time.

我們認識很久了！

深入分析

each other是彼此、互相，know each other則是彼此互相認識的意思。

應用會話

A: John, have you ever met Susan?
約翰，你有見過蘇珊嗎？

B: Yes,we've known each other for a long time.
有的，我們認識很久了！

A: You talked to each other, didn't you?
你們有彼此交談過，不是嗎？

B: Yes, we did.
有的，我們是有啊！

類似用法

☞ I've known David for a long time.
我已經認識大衛很久了！

基本用語

Track 094

Here's my bus.

我等的公車來了!

深入分析

當你在等公車的同時，又正和熟人在聊天，此時公車到站了，你就可以說:"Here's my bus."字面意思是「這裡是我的公車」，其實就是公車抵達了、我準備道別的意思。

應用會話

A: That's right. Oh, here's my bus.
沒錯! 喔，我的公車來了!

B: That's my bus too.
那也是我的公車。

A: Oh, here's my bus. See you around.
喔，我的公車來了!再見囉!

B: Good-bye.
再見!

基本用語

Track 095

It's not good for your health.

那對你的健康不好!

深入分析

若是對方所做的行為，對他自己是有害的，就可以告誡對方:"It's not good for you."，若特別是對他的健康有損，就可以說:"It's not good for your health."

應用會話

A: You look terrible. What's wrong?
你看起來糟透了! 怎麼啦?

B: I was up late last night.
我昨晚太晚睡了。

A: It's not good for your health.
那對你的健康不好!

A: It's not good for your health.
那對你的健康不好!

B: I know, but I have to finish the sales report in time.
我知道，但是我要及時完成銷售報告。

基本用語

Track 096

I have to go.

我要走了。

深入分析

have to go是必須要走了，也就是準備要離開前的預告用語，表示自己打算要結束目前正在討論的話題，即將準備離去的意思。

應用會話

A: I have to go.
我要走了。

B: Sure. See you soon.
好！再見囉！

A: Can't you stay for dinner?
你不能留下來吃晚餐嗎？

B: Sorry. I really have to go.
抱歉，我真的要走了。

類似用法

☞ I've got to go.
我必須要走了。

☞ I'll be leaving.
我要離開了。

基本用語

Track 097

Have you ever been to Paris?

你有去過巴黎嗎?

深入分析

當你要詢問對方是否到過某地時，要用完成式的句型，此時就可以說："Have you ever been to somewhere"，been是動詞be的過去分詞。

應用會話

A: Have you ever been to Paris?
你有去過巴黎嗎?

B: Yes, I have.
有的，我有過。

A: Have you ever been to Japan?
你有去過日本嗎?

B: No, I have never been there before.
沒有，我以前沒有去過那裡。

基本用語

Track 098

Yes, please.

好的，謝謝!

深入分析

當對方問你是否需要某物（例如點餐、接受幫助），你就可以禮貌性的回應:"Yes, please."，表示你願意，並有謝謝、麻煩對方的意思，若是拒絕，則可以說"No, thanks."。

應用會話

A: Coffee?
要喝咖啡嗎?

B: Yes, please.
好的，謝謝!

A: Would you like a cup of coffee?
要不要喝一杯咖啡?

B: Yes, please.
好的，謝謝!

A: Want something to drink?
想喝點什麼嗎?

B: No, thanks.
不用，謝謝!

基本用語

Track 099

I'm sorry to hear that.

聽到這件事我很遺憾。

深入分析

當對方告知你發生不好的事情時，你就可以抱持同理心告訴對方你感同身受，並覺得遺憾。

應用會話

A: David is seeing someone else.
大衛和其他人約會。

B: I'm sorry to hear that.
聽到這件事我很遺憾。

A: You know what? I'm really angry.
你知道嗎？我真的很生氣！

B: I'm sorry to hear that.
聽到這件事我很遺憾。

類似用法

☞ I'm so shocked to hear that.
聽到這件事我相當的震驚！

☞ So sorry to hear that.
很遺憾知道這件事！

基本用語

Track 100

That's too bad!

真糟糕!

深入分析

發生糟糕、令人惋惜或不幸的事件時，最常用的遺憾用語是: "That's too bad!"，也可以說"Too bad!"。

應用會話

A: I was laid off.
我被資遣了。

B: Gee, that's too bad!
唉呀!真是太糟了啊!

A: That's too bad! I've got a flat tire.
真糟糕!爆胎了。

B: What shall we do now?
我們現在該怎麼辦?

基本用語

Track 101

How unfortunate!

真不幸啊!

深入分析

若是聽見不幸或不好的消息，甚至感到惋惜時，就可以說："How unfortunate!"。

應用會話

A: I had a car accident.
我發生車禍了!

B: How unfortunate!
真不幸啊!

A: I got fired.
我被炒魷魚了。

B: How unfortunate!
真不幸啊!

A: I think I failed my math test.
我想我搞砸了數學考試。

B: How unfortunate!
真不幸啊!

基本用語

Track 102

How awful!

真是太可怕了！

深入分析

若是發生令人感到害怕或嚴重的事件時，請感同身受的說："How awful!"。

應用會話

A: I might have broken a bone.
我可能骨折了。

B: How awful!
真是太可怕了！

A: My bag was snatched last night.
昨晚我的袋子被搶了！

B: How awful!
真是太可怕了！

A: How awful!
真是太可怕了！

B: Yes, it is.
沒錯，的確是！

基本用語

Track 103

That's a pity.

真可惜!

深入分析

發生令人感到惋惜的事件時，也可以說:"That's a pity."，表示太可惜了!

應用會話

A: My score is not good enough.
我的成績不夠好。

B: That's a pity.
真可惜!

A: It's my fault.
是我的錯。

B: That's a pity.
真可惜!

類似用法

☞ What a shame!
真是可惜!

基本用語

Track 104

What bad luck!

運氣真是差呀！

深入分析

若對方運氣不好，老是遇上不如意的事，就可以替對方感到遺憾："What bad luck!"。

應用會話

A: I shouldn't have gone to see a movie last week.
我上星期不應該去看電影。

B: What bad luck!
運氣真是差呀！

A: How do you do, Jack?
你好嗎，傑克?

B: Not so good. I broke my leg.
不太好。我摔斷腿了！

A: What bad luck!
運氣真是差呀！

基本用語

I hope it's nothing serious.

希望情況不會太嚴重。

深入分析

若對方發生不好的事，你可以客套的安慰、期待這件事不要太嚴重:"I hope it's nothing serious."，字面意思是「沒有事情是嚴重的」，表示希望人都平安的意思。

應用會話

A: I hope it's nothing serious.
希望情況不會太嚴重。

B: Don't try to comfort me.
不用試圖安慰我。

A: I had a car accident last week.
我上星期發生了車禍。

B: I hope it's nothing serious.
希望情況不會太嚴重。

A: Don't worry about me.
不要擔心我。

基本用語

Track 106

Sorry for that.

我為那件事感到抱歉啦!

深入分析

sorry可以是道歉、遺憾的意思，sorry for something表示為某事感到遺憾、抱歉的意思，that是指特定你我所知道的那件事。

應用會話

A: I didn't mean to.
我不是故意的。

B: It's OK!
沒關係!

A: Sorry for that.
我為那件事感到抱歉啦!

A: Sorry for that.
我為那件事感到抱歉啦!

B: Hey, nothing is happening.
喂，沒事啦!

基本用語

Track 107

Good to hear that.

很高興聽見這件事。

深入分析

當你聽到或知道了某件事，並為對方感到高興時，就可以說:"Good to hear that."，全文是"It's good to hear that."

應用會話

A: Hi, John. Come on in.
嗨，約翰!進來吧!

B: How is school?
學校還好嗎?

A: Pretty good.
很好!

B: Good to hear that.
很高興聽見這件事。

類似用法

☞ I'm glad to hear that.
很高興聽你這麼說。

基本用語

Track 108

Thank you.

謝謝你。

深入分析

表達謝意的最基本語句就是:"Thank you."，若要更周到，可以在句子後面加上對方的名字，例如"Thank you, David."。

應用會話

A: Here you are.
給你。

B: Thank you. I appreciate that.
謝謝你。真的很感激你!

A: Thank you. You've been very helpful.
謝謝你。你幫了一個大忙。

B: Don't mention it.
不必客氣!

類似用法

☞ Thank you very much.
非常感謝。

☞ Thanks a lot.
多謝了。

基本用語

Track 109

Thank you anyway.

總之，還是很謝謝你!

深入分析

若是對方很願意幫忙，但卻半點使不上力時，你仍需要感謝對方，中文會說:「不管怎樣，還是謝謝你!」英文就是"Thank you anyway."

應用會話

A: I did all I could do.
我已經盡力而為了。

B: Thank you anyway.
總之，還是很謝謝你!

A: Keeping busy? Give me a hand.
在忙嗎? 幫幫我。

B: But I'm in the middle of something, sorry.
但是我現在正在忙，抱歉。

A: It's OK. Thank you anyway.
沒關係!總之，還是很謝謝你!

基本用語

Track 110

No, thanks.

不用，謝謝！

深入分析

當對方主動提供協助，但你自覺可以自己處理時，別忘了基本的禮儀喔："No, thanks." 表示我不用你的幫助，但還是要謝謝你！

應用會話

A: Do you want a ride?
要搭我的便車嗎?

B: No, thanks. I don't want to bother you.
不用，謝謝！我不想麻煩你！

A: How about having some sponge cake?
要不要吃一些海綿蛋糕?

B: No, thanks. I'm on a diet.
不用，謝謝！我在節食中！

類似用法

☞ Thank you all the same.
還是得謝謝你。

基本用語

Track 111

Thank you for your concern.

謝謝你的關心。

深入分析

對方主動關心你的狀況時，也不要忘記謝謝對方的關心："Thank you for your concern."

應用會話

A: David, are you OK?
大衛，你還好吧?

B: Just fine. Thank you for your concern.
還可以!謝謝你的關心。

A: Don't worry about it. He'll be fine.
不用擔心!他會沒事的。

B: Thank you for your concern.
謝謝你的關心。

基本用語

Track 112

Thanks again for everything.

這一切真的要很感謝你!

深入分析

對方提供了相當多的協助，你可能已經道謝過了，到了最後要道別或分離時，你還是想要再道謝一次以表達自己的感激之情，就可以說："Thanks again for everything."

應用會話

A: Don't forget to keep in touch.
不要忘記要保持聯絡!

B: Thanks again for everything.
這一切真的要很感謝你!

A: It's no big deal.
沒什麼大不了!

A: I trust you. Don't worry about it.
我相信你!不要擔心。

B: Thanks again for everything.
這一切真的要很感謝你!

基本用語

Track 113

Thank you for all you did.

感謝你所做的一切！

深入分析

對方盡心盡力提供協助，你可以針對這樣的所作所為，提出你的感謝之情："Thank you for all you did."通常後面要加you did表示所做過的事。

應用會話

A: Thank you for all you did.
感謝你所做的一切！

B: Come on. What are friends for?
別這麼說！朋友就是要互相幫忙！

A: You can make it.
你辦得到的！

B: I know. Thank you for all you did.
我知道！感謝你所做的一切！

類似用法

☞ Thank you for all you've done for me.
感謝你為我所做的一切！

基本用語

Track 114

It's really nice of you.

你真是太好了。

深入分析

雖然沒有道謝，但是對方的好心、親切卻讓你非常感動，就可以說："It's really nice of you."。

應用會話

A: I'm sure it's no problem.
我確定沒問題啦!

B: It's really nice of you.
你真是太好了。

A: It's really nice of you.
你真是太好了。

B: It's no big deal, right?
沒什麼大不了，對吧?

類似用法

☞ That's really kind of you.
你真是太好了!

☞ You are so kind.
你真好心!

基本用語

Track 115

I appreciate that.

我很感激！

深入分析

道謝(Thank you)之後，你可以說「我真的很感激！」英文就叫做："I appreciate that."，以凸顯你道地的英文用語。

應用會話

A: Please let me know if there's anything I can do.
如果我能做點什麼，請告訴我。

B: Thanks. I appreciate that.
謝謝！我很感激！

A: Let me help you.
我來幫你。

B: Thanks. I appreciate that.
謝謝！ 我很感激！

類似用法

☞ I really appreciate that.
我真的很感激！

基本用語

Track 116

You're welcome.

不必客氣！

深入分析

對方向你道謝之後，你就應該禮貌回應，英文就叫做"You're welcome."，字面意思是歡迎的，也就是「不必客氣！」的意思。

應用會話

A: You've been really helpful.
你真的幫了大忙。

B: You're welcome.
不必客氣！

A: Thank you anyway.
總之還是謝謝你！

B: You're welcome.
不必客氣！

類似用法

☞ That's OK.
不必客氣。

基本用語

Track 117

Don't mention it.

不必客氣!

深入分析

「不必客氣!」除了"You're welcome."之外，還可以說"Don't mention it."，字面意思「不用提及」，也就是「不必客氣!」的意思。

應用會話

A: Thank you so much.
謝謝你。你真的幫了大忙!

B: Don't mention it.
不必客氣!

A: You've been very helpful.
你真的幫了大忙!

B: Don't mention it.
不必客氣!

類似用法

☞ No problem.
不必客氣!

☞ That's all right.
不必客氣!

基本用語

Track 118

You have us.

你有我們（陪你）啊！

深入分析

當對方面對困境時，你也願意幫助對方度過難關時，可以這麼安慰對方："You have us."，表示不管如何，我們都會陪著你的意思，通常表示有多人支持就用us，若只有你自己一個人，就用me。

應用會話

A: What shall I do?
我該怎麼辦?

B: You have us.
你有我們（陪你）啊！

A: It's good to have you here.
有你們真好！

A: I don't know what to do.
我不知道要怎麼做。

B: You have us.
你有我們（陪你）啊！

基本用語

Track 119

I'll be here with you.

我會陪你度過一切!

深入分析

面對有困境的人，只要告訴對方:「我會在這裡陪你」，你的陪伴，是能夠讓對方在心理上有個可以依靠的靠山!

應用會話

A: But what shall I do?
但我應該怎麼做?

B: I'll be here with you.
我會陪你度過一切!

A: I'll be here with you.
我會陪你度過一切!

B: It's good to have you here.
有你真好!

A: I can't believe it happened to me.
我不敢相信這會發生在我身上。

B: Don't worry. I'll be here with you.
別擔心，我會陪你度過一切。

基本用語

Track 120

It's good to have you here.

有你在真好!

深入分析

當你面對困難時，一定會希望有人能夠在你身旁陪伴你度過一切，那麼你要如何感謝對方呢?你可以說:"It's good to have you here."表示「真高興你(們)在這裡陪我」的意思。

應用會話

A: Please let me know if there's anything I can do.
如果我能做點什麼，請告訴我。

B: Thanks. It's good to have you here.
謝謝! 有你在真好!

A: Could you bring me a glass of hot water?
可以幫我倒一杯熱水嗎?

B: Here you are.
來，給你!

A: Thanks. It's good to have you here.
謝謝! 有你在真好!

基本用語

Track 121

Let me know if there's anything I can do.

如果我能做點什麼，請告訴我。

深入分析

若你願意主動提供協助，就應該告訴對方："Let me know if there's anything I can do."，表示你什麼都願意做，也就是不吝嗇幫助的意思。

應用會話

A: Let me know if there's anything I can do.
如果我能做點什麼，請告訴我。

B: Thanks. I feel much better now.
謝謝！現在我覺得好多了。

A: Let me know if there's anything I can do.
如果我能做點什麼，請告訴我。

B: What's your opinion?
你的意見呢?

類似用法

☞ Let me know if there is anything I can do for you.
如果我能為你做什麼，請告訴我。

基本用語

Track 122

You are really thoughtful.

你真是太周到了。

深入分析

thoughtful是思想縝密、細心的意思，通常是因為對方有體貼的行為，而你很感激的回覆用語。

應用會話

A: You are really thoughtful.
你真是太周到了。

B: It's no big deal.
沒什麼大不了。

A: If I can do anything, just let me know.
如果我能做些什麼，請告訴我。

B: Thanks. You are really thoughtful.
謝謝！你真是太周到了。

基本用語

Track 123

Do you need anything?

你有需要什麼東西嗎?

深入分析

當對方明顯看起來需要某事協助時，你就可以主動關心，表示自己可以想辦法協助提供的意思。

應用會話

A: I feel so cold.
我覺得好冷!

B: Do you need anything?
你有需要什麼東西嗎?

A: Could you bring me a glass of hot water?
可以幫我倒一杯熱水嗎?

B: Sure. Here you are.
當然好!給你!

A: Are you OK?
你還好吧?

B: No, I am not.
不，一點都不好。

A: Do you need anything?
你有需要什麼東西嗎?

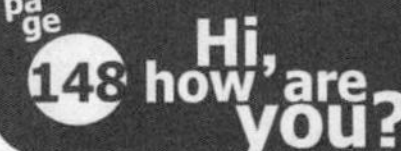

基本用語

Track 124

Where have you been?

你都去哪啦?

深入分析

當你想要知道對方去過哪些地方時，就可以問："Where have you been?"，也帶有問對方最近失蹤了一陣子後，做了哪些事的意味。

應用會話

A: Where have you been?
你都去哪啦?

B: I've been away doing shopping.
我出去買東西了。

A: Where have you been?
你都去哪啦?

B: I've been away on vacation.
我出去度假了。

A: Where have you been?
你都去哪啦?

B: I've been away on a business trip.
我去出差了。

基本用語

Track 125

I guess.

我猜測的!

深入分析

當你發表了某些言論，卻又不是那麼確認真實性時，就可以在句尾補上一句:"I guess."，表示自己不是那麼確定，一切都是猜測的意思。

應用會話

A: Are you OK, David?
大衛，你還好吧?

B: I don't know. I twisted my back, I guess.
不知道耶。我猜我扭傷我的背了。

A: When will Mr. Jones be free?
瓊斯先生什麼時候會有空?

B: He won't have a break until two o'clock, I guess.
我猜一直到兩點鐘之前他都不會有空。

基本用語

Track 126

Let me have a look.

我看一下。

深入分析

表明自己希望能察看某個事物時，就可以說"have a look"，look是察看的意思。

應用會話

A: Let me have a look.
我看一下。

B: Well?
怎麼樣?

A: It looks terrible.
看起來很嚴重。

A: I think I twisted my back.
我想我扭傷背了。

B: Let me have a look.
我看一下。

類似用法

☞ Let me take a look.
給我看一下!

☞ May I have a look?
我可以看一下嗎?

基本用語

Track 127

It hurts.

會很痛!

深入分析

表示疼痛就用hurt。"It hurts."可以表示身體任何部位或原因所造成的疼痛現象。

應用會話

A: How do you feel now?
你現在覺得如何?

B: It hurts.
很痛!

A: Stop touching my back. It hurts.
不要碰我的背了。會很痛!

B: You gotta get that looked at, honey.
親愛的，你真的需要去檢查一下。

基本用語

Track 128

How long have you had it?

這樣的狀況有多久了?

深入分析

當對方有某種症狀，特別是有問題或不好的狀況時，你就可以關心對方這樣的情形持續多久了:"How long have you had it?"。

應用會話

A: How long have you had it?
這樣的狀況有多久了?

B: Since this Wednesday.
從這個星期三開始。

A: How long have you had it?
這樣的狀況有多久了?

B: Four days, I guess.
我想有四天了!

基本用語

Track 129

Is that so serious?

有這麼嚴重?

深入分析

若是情況看起來很嚴重，就可以用疑問的語氣問:"Is that so serious?"，表示你想要知道，是否如你所猜測或看到的現象一樣嚴重。

應用會話

A: It looks terrible.
看起來很糟糕!

B: Is that so serious?
有這麼嚴重?

A: Is that so serious?
有這麼嚴重?

B: No, not at all.
不，不會啦!

基本用語

Track 130

I really need to take a break.

我真的需要休息一 下!

深入分析

take a break是指短暫休息一段時間的意思，通常適用在從事某件事一段很長的時間後，稍事休息時使用。

應用會話

A: You look tired.
你看起來很累耶!

B: Yeah, I really need to take a break.
是啊! 我真的需要休息一 下!

A: I really need to take a break.
我真的需要休息一 下!

B: Good for you.
對你來說是好事!

A: You look tired.
你看起來很累。

B: I really need to take a break.
我真的需要休息一下。

基本用語

Track 131

Would you like a cup of coffee?

要不要喝一杯咖啡?

深入分析

"Would you like..."是禮貌性問句，表示詢問對方是否想要某事物的意思，後面通常加名詞。

應用會話

A: Would you like a cup of coffee?
要不要喝一杯咖啡?

B: Yes, please.
好的，謝謝!

A: Would you like a cup of coffee?
要不要喝一杯咖啡?

B: No, thanks.
不用了，謝謝!

類似用法

☞ Coffee?
要喝咖啡嗎?

☞ Would you like some tea?
要不要喝杯茶?

☞ Tea or coffee?
要喝茶或咖啡?

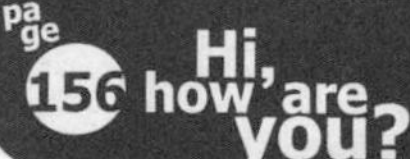

基本用語

Track 132

Would you like something to drink?

要不要來點飲料?

深入分析

直接問對方想喝點什麼的問句就可以說:"Would you like something to drink?",something可以泛指任何想喝(to drink)的飲料。

應用會話

A: Would you like something to drink?
要不要來點飲料?

B: I'd like a cup of tea, please.
我要喝一杯茶,謝謝。

A: Would you like something to drink?
要不要來點飲料?

B: No, thanks.
不用了,謝謝!

基本用語

Track 133

I'm on a diet.

我在節食中!

深入分析

on a diet是控制飲食或節食的意思。當對方鼓勵你多吃一點時，你就可以說:"I'm on a diet."，表示拒絕、不願再進食的意思。

應用會話

A: How about having some sponge cake?
要不要吃一些海綿蛋糕?

B: No, thanks. I'm on a diet.
不用，謝謝!我在節食中!

A: You look great.
你看起來氣色真好。

B: Really? I'm on a diet.
真的嗎? 我在節食中!

基本用語

Track 134

What did you have for dinner?

你們晚餐吃了什麼?

深入分析

have是擁有，也可以當成進食、吃東西的動詞。for dinner是當成晚餐的意思。for後面可以加上三餐的名稱，表示當成某餐餐點的意思。

應用會話

A: What did you have for dinner?
你們晚餐吃了什麼?

B: We ate some sandwiches for dinner.
我們晚餐吃了些三明治。

A: What did you have for dinner?
你們晚餐吃什麼?

B: As usual, I had bread and eggs.
我照例吃了麵包和雞蛋。

A: What did you havc for breakfast?
你早上吃了什麼?

B: I had bread for breakfast.
我早餐吃麵包。

基本用語

Track 135

Here you are.

來，給你!

深入分析

當你要拿某物給對方時，中文會說「給你」，英文就叫做:"Here you are."，表示「這個是要給你的東西，請接手」。

應用會話

A: Black coffee?
要黑咖啡嗎?

B: That's right.
沒錯!

A: Here you are.
來，給你!

A: Here you are.
來，給你!

B: Thanks a lot.
多謝囉!

基本用語

Track 136

Are you serious?

你是認真的嗎?

深入分析

表示要確認對方是否是認真的態度時的詢問語句。serious是嚴肅、認真的意思。

應用會話

A: I'm going to marry Jane.
我要和珍結婚。

B: I can't believe it. Are you serious?
真是不敢相信!你是認真的嗎?

A: Yes, I am.
是的,我是認真的!

A: Are you serious?
你是認真的嗎?

B: Sure.
當然啊!

類似用法

☞ Are you serious about it?
你對這件事是認真的嗎?

基本用語

Track 137

I'm serious.

我是認真的！

深入分析

表示自己的言行並不是開玩笑，所言所行都是經過深思熟慮的，且是認真的態度。

應用會話

A: We were separated.
我們分居了！

B: Are you kidding me?
你是開玩笑的吧？

A: No, I'm serious.
不，我是認真的。

類似用法

☞ I meant it.
我是認真的。

☞ I'm not kidding.
我不是開玩笑的。

☞ It's not a joke.
這不是開玩笑的！

基本用語

Track 138

You can't be serious!

你不是認真的吧?

深入分析

雖是否定用法，但其實是表示自己不敢相信對方的言行，直覺認為對方是開玩笑的、不可能是認真的的意思。

應用會話

A: You can't be serious!
你不是認真的吧?

B: Why not?
為什麼不是?

A: I'm going to attend that meeting.
我要去參加那場會議。

B: You can't be serious!
你不是認真的吧?

A: Yes, I am.
是的，我就是。

基本用語

Track 139

Are you sure?

你確定嗎?

深入分析

想要確認對方的言行，通常適用在你聽到令人不敢相信的事件後的反應。

應用會話

A: Could we meet at four thirty?
我們能在四點卅分見面嗎?

B: Are you sure?
你確定嗎?

A: Why don't we talk to David about it?
我們為什麼不和大衛談一談呢?

B: Are you sure?
你確定嗎?

A: Of course.
當然!

類似用法

☞ Are you sure about it?
你確定?

基本用語

Track 140

I'm not sure.

我不確定。

表示連自己都無法確認或肯定的意思。

應用會話

A: Do you know where Kenny is?
你知道肯尼在哪裡嗎?

B: Sorry, I'm not sure.
對不起，我不太清楚。

類似用法

☞ I'm not so sure.
我不是那麼確定。

☞ I'm not sure about it.
我不太確定。

☞ I'm not quite sure.
我不太確定。

基本用語

Track 141

No kidding.

不是開玩笑的吧!

深入分析

認為所聽聞的事物應該都是玩笑話、不是認真的意思，也表示自己不相信這一切。

應用會話

A: What are you going to do?
你打算怎麼作?

B: I have no idea. It depends on the situation.
我不知道。要視情況而定。

A: No kidding.
不是開玩笑的吧!

A: No kidding.
不是開玩笑的吧!

B: Could be, but I'm not so sure.
有可能，但是我不確定。

基本用語

Track 142

I'm kidding.

我是開玩笑的!

深入分析

希望對方不必那麼認真,自己的言行都是開玩笑、取樂對方的意思。

應用會話

A: Are you sure?
你確定嗎?

B: I'm kidding.
我是開玩笑的!

A: How unfortunate!
多不幸啊!

B: Come on, buddy, I'm kidding.
兄弟,不要這樣啦!我是開玩笑的!

A: I'm kidding.
我是開玩笑的。

B: Not funny.
不好笑!

基本用語

Track 143

You must be kidding.

你是在開玩笑的吧！

深入分析

想要知道對方是認真的，還是一切都只是個嬉鬧的玩笑。

應用會話

A: I got married yesterday.
我昨天結婚了。

B: What? You must be kidding.
什麼？你是在開玩笑的吧！

A: You must be kidding.
你是在開玩笑的吧！

B: It's true.
是真的！

類似用法

☞ No kidding?
不是開玩笑的吧！

☞ Are you kidding me?
你在跟我開玩笑吧？

☞ Is that a joke?
是開玩笑的嗎？

基本用語

Track 144

You asked for it.

是你自己找罪受!

深入分析

表示對於對方目前所遭受的狀況不值得同情，因為是對方自作自受的意思。

應用會話

A: I can't believe that it happened to me.
不敢相信這件事發生在我身上。

B: You asked for it.
是你自己找罪受!

A: I'm counting on David to solve it.
我依賴大衛來解決這件事。

B: Sure. You asked for it.
當然啊!是你自己找罪受!

類似用法

☞ You're asking for it.
你是自找的!

基本用語

Track 145

You really think so?

你真的這麼認為?

深入分析

反問對方是否是真的抱持某種想法或觀念的意思。so代表所聽聞的事件。

應用會話

A: You really think so?
你真的這麼認為?

B: Yes, I do. Why not?
是的，我是! 為什麼不可以?

A: Maybe we should take some food to the party.
也許我們應該帶一些食物到派對。

B: You really think so?
你真的這麼認為?

A: Yes, I do. OK. Let's go now.
是的，我是!好吧!我們走!

基本用語

Track 146

I see.

我了解了！

深入分析

字面意思是「我看見」，但其實就是「我瞭解」、「我明白」的意思，多適用在回應對方的說明。

應用會話

A: I won't invite David to the concert.
我不會邀請大衛去聽音樂會。

B: I see.
我了解了！

A: That's the reason why I have to call her.
那就是為什麼我要打電話給她的理由。

B: Oh, I see.
喔！我瞭解了。

類似用法

☞ I got it.
我了解了！

☞ I understand.
我了解了！

基本用語

Track 147

I got you.

我懂你的意思。

深入分析

字面意思是「我得到你」，其實就是「我瞭解你的想法或說明」的意思。

應用會話

A: I think Taipei is a fashionable city.
我覺得台北是一個流行的城市。

B: I got you.
我懂你的意思。

A: I have had to postpone the Annual Sales Conference.
我必須把年度銷售會議延期。

B: I got you.
我懂你的意思。

類似用法

☞ I see what you mean.
我了解你的意思。

基本用語

Track 148

I don't get it.

我不懂！

深入分析

字面意思是無法得到，也就是表示自己不瞭解、不懂的意思。

應用會話

A: Is that clear to you?
這樣你清楚了嗎？

B: Sorry, I still don't get it!
抱歉，我還是不明白！

類似用法

☞ I still don't get it!
我還是不明白！

☞ I don't see the point.
我不明白。

☞ I don't get the picture.
我不明白。

☞ I don't understand.
我不瞭解。

基本用語

Track 149

I didn't catch you.

我沒有聽懂你的意思!

深入分析

字面意思是沒有抓到你，其實在對方發表某些言論後，你還是不懂時，就可以說："I didn't catch you."。

應用會話

A: Do you hear me?
聽懂我的意思了嗎?

B: I didn't catch you.
我沒有聽懂你的意思!

A: So we've decided to finish it.
所以我們已經決定要完成它了!

B: Sorry, I didn't catch you.
抱歉，我沒有聽懂!

基本用語

Track 150

I'm confused.

我被搞得糊里糊塗的!

深入分析

表示自己目前毫無頭緒、思緒被搞混的意思。若是事物令人糊塗，則為"It's confusing."。

應用會話

A: I'm confused.
我被搞得糊里糊塗的!

B: You still didn't get it, did you?
你還是沒弄懂，對吧?

A: No, I didn't.
沒有，我沒弄懂!

類似用法

☞ I'm a bit confused.
我有點被搞得有點糊里糊塗的!

基本用語

Track 151

You're confusing me!

你把我搞得糊里糊塗的。

深入分析

表示是因為對方的緣故，導致自己搞不清楚狀況的意思。

應用會話

A: You're confusing me!
你把我搞得糊里糊塗的。

B: You really think so?
你真的這麼認為?

A: I'm tired of being a good student.
我對當一個乖乖牌學生感到厭煩了。

B: What? You're confusing me!
什麼啊? 你把我搞得糊里糊塗的。

基本用語

Track 152

I'm proud of you.

我為你感到驕傲。

深入分析

常常可以看見這樣的情節，作父母的為了子女擁有高成就而感到驕傲，此時他們最常說的一句話就是："I'm proud of you."表示「我以你為榮。」

應用會話

A: I got through the task as quickly as possible.
我盡快地完成了工作。

B: Good. I'm proud of you.
很好！我為你感到驕傲。

A: I finished the sales plan on my own.
我獨力完成這份銷售計畫。

B: Really? I'm so proud of you.
真的？我非常以你為榮。

基本用語

Track 153

You must be proud of yourself.

你一定為自己感到驕傲。

深入分析

當然也可以為自己感到驕傲，就叫做"be proud of one's self"。若是多人的「你們自己」，則是yourselves。

應用會話

A: I finished my report in time.
我有如期完成我的報告！

B: You must be proud of yourself.
你一定為自己感到驕傲。

A: We won.
我們贏了！

B: You must be proud of yourselves.
你們一定為自己感到驕傲。

基本用語

Track 154

You really make me proud.

你真的讓我感到驕傲。

深入分析

令某人感到驕傲，就可以說"make someone proud"。

應用會話

A: You really make me proud.
你真的讓我感到驕傲。

B: Of course. I think it's a good chance.
當然啊！我覺得這是一個好機會。

A: I have to do it by myself.
我應該自己去做這件事。

B: I see. You really make me proud.
我了解了。你真的讓我感到驕傲。

基本用語

Track 155

I'm tired of it.

我對它感到很厭煩了。

深入分析

對某事物感到厭煩時，就可以使用"be tired of..."，tired是疲累的，但也有「厭煩的」之意。

應用會話

A: I'm tired of it.
我對它感到很厭煩了。

B: Maybe you should talk to the manager.
也許你應該告訴主管。

A: So which side are you?
所以你要站在哪一方?

B: Whatever! I'm tired of it.
不管了！我對它感到很厭煩了。

類似用法

☞ I'm fed up with it.
我對它煩死了！

基本用語

Track 156

I'm sick of it.

噁心死了！

"be sick of..."可不是生病的意思，而是對某事感到噁心的意思。

應用會話

A: I'm sick of it.
噁心死了！

B: Why? What happened to you?
為什麼？你怎麼啦？

A: I'm sick of it.
噁心死了！

B: Are you kidding me?
你是開玩笑的吧？

A: No, I'm serious.
不，我是認真的。

基本用語

Track 157

This is too much!

真是太過份了！

深入分析

too much的字面意思是「太多」，也就是某人或某事太超過、過份，而令人感到不滿的情緒抗議。

應用會話

A: They didn't tell me anything.
他們什麼也沒有告訴我。

B: This is too much!
真是太過份了！

A: Tracy is a gossip.
崔西愛搬弄是非。

B: This is too much!
真是太過份了！

基本用語

Track 158

I hate this.

我恨死這一切了。

深入分析

表示極度討厭這一切的意思。this就是和對話方所討論的這一事件。

應用會話

A: I hate this.
我恨死這一切了。

B: Come on, it's just a joke.
得了吧!只是個玩笑。

A: I hate this.
我恨死這一切了。

B: It won't make me change my mind.
我都不會改變主意的。

A: You are fired?
你被炒魷魚了?

B: Yeah! I hate this.
是啊! 我恨死這一切了。

基本用語

Track 159

Be quiet.

安靜！

深入分析

要對方安靜一點、不要打擾到人時的用法。這是禮貌性的要求安靜用法，另一種較為無禮地要他人閉嘴的說法是"Shut up."。

應用會話

A: Be quiet.
安靜！

B: I'm sorry to bother you.
很抱歉打擾你。

A: Be quiet.
安靜！

B: Sure. Sorry.
好的！抱歉！

類似用法

☞ Shut up.
閉嘴！

基本用語

Track 160

Did I bother you?

我有打擾到你嗎?

深入分析

不確定自己是否有造成對方的麻煩，因此而提出問句以確認的意思。

應用會話

A: Jack?
傑克?

B: Did I bother you?
我有打擾你嗎?

A: Not at all. Come on in.
沒有啊！進來吧！

A: Did I bother you?
我有打擾你嗎?

B: What do you think?
你覺得呢?

A: Did I bother you?
我有打擾你嗎?

B: Yes, you did.
是的，你有。

基本用語

Track 161

I'm sorry to bother you.

很抱歉打擾你。

深入分析

因為自己做了某些事（大部分是不好的事或引起麻煩的事），自己為此致歉的用語。

應用會話

A: I'm sorry to bother you.
很抱歉打擾你。

B: Don't worry about it. We were just having dinner.
不用擔心!我們剛吃過晚餐!

A: I'm sorry to bother you. Got a minute to talk?
很抱歉打擾你。現在有空談一談嗎?

B: Sure. What's up?
當然有啊!什麼事?

類似用法

☞ Sorry to bother you.
很抱歉打擾你。

基本用語

Track 162

Don't bother me.

不要來打擾我！

深入分析

要求對方不要來打擾自己，通常是一種直接、較無禮的說法。

應用會話

A: Don't bother me.
不要來打擾我！

B: Oh, sorry.
喔，抱歉！

A: Busy?
忙嗎？

B: Yup! Don't bother me.
是啊！不要來打擾我！

類似用法

☞ Leave me alone.
不要來煩我！

基本用語

Please don't bother.

不必麻煩你了!

當對方提出要主動幫你做某事，你基於某些原因拒絕時，可以告訴對方「不用麻煩你了!」英文就叫做"Please don't bother."。

A: Let me drive you home.
我開車載你回家。

B: Please don't bother.
不必麻煩你了!

A: Let me take a look for you.
我來幫你看看!

B: Please don't bother.
不必麻煩你了!

類似用法

☞ Don't bother.
不必麻煩了!

基本用語

Track 164

It really bothers me.

這讓我很困擾！

深入分析

表示某事造成自己的困擾的意思，雖沒有說明哪件事，但用it表示兩人有默契都知道的事。

應用會話

A: It really bothers me.
這讓我很困擾！

B: What's the matter?
發生什麼事？

A: Did I say something wrong?
我說錯話了嗎？

B: Yeah! And it really bothers me.
是啊，而且這讓我很困擾！

基本用語

Track 165

It's not necessary.

沒有必要啦!

深入分析

表示沒有必要、不必麻煩的意思時,就可以說:"It's not necessary."。

應用會話

A: If you need any help, just let me know, OK?
如果你需要任何幫助,請讓我知道,好嗎?

B: Thanks! It's not necessary.
謝謝! 沒有必要啦!

A: Let's all get together again.
讓我們再聚會一次吧!

B: It's not necessary.
沒有必要啦!

基本用語

Track 166

Can you manage it by yourself?

你可以自己處理嗎?

深入分析

manage是「管理」，整句話的意思是「你可以自己做」，通常你的回答若是不可以，對方就會提供協助的意思。

應用會話

A: Can you manage it by yourself?
你可以自己處理嗎?

B: Yeah. Don't bother.
是啊!不必麻煩你了!

A: Can you manage it by yourself?
你可以自己處理嗎?

B: Well... I don't think so.
嗯，可能不行吧!

類似用法

☞ Allow me, sir.
先生，讓我來處理!

☞ Allow me, madam.
女士，讓我來處理!

基本用語

Track 167

I can handle this by myself.

我可以自己處理。

深入分析

通常是對方表示要主動提供協助，但你卻可以自己處理、無須對方協助的回應，表示含蓄地拒絕接受幫助之意。

應用會話

A: Let me know if you need help.
如果你需要幫助，讓我知道一下。

B: No problem. I can handle this by myself.
沒問題的！我可以自己處理。

A: Do you need help?
你需要幫助嗎？

B: No, thanks. I can handle this by myself.
不用，謝謝！我可以自己處理。

基本用語

Track 168

Oh, boy!

天啊！

深入分析

當發生令人高興、訝異、吃驚或不敢相信的事時，就可以說摀著胸口說："Boy!"

應用會話

A: Oh, boy! He is so cute.
天啊！他真是帥啊！

B: You really think so?
你真的這麼認為？

A: Check this out.
你看！

B: Oh, boy! I can't believe it.
天啊！我真是不敢相信！

類似用法

☞ Boy, oh boy!
天啊！

☞ My God.
我的天啊！

☞ Man!
我的天啊！

基本用語

Track 169

There you go again!

你又來了！

深入分析

可能是對方老是做某事（通常是負面的事件）時，當對方又出現這樣的行為時，你就可以說:"There you go again!"，通常是表示不滿或抗議的意思。

應用會話

A: There you go again!
你又來了！

B: But I really mean it.
我是說真的！

A: There you go again!
你又來了！

B: So what?
那又怎麼樣?

A: There you go again!
你又來了！

B: I can't help it.
我情不自禁！

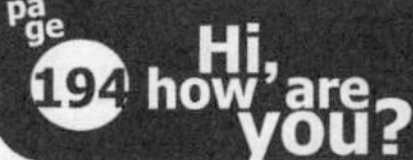

基本用語

Track 170

Keep in touch.

要保持聯絡喔!

深入分析

道別時的用語，希望對方能和自己保持密切的聯絡。

應用會話

A: Keep in touch.
要保持聯絡喔!

B: Sure. Bye!
當然囉！再見!

A: Take care of yourself.
好好照顧自己!

B: Yeah. Keep in touch.
好啊！要保持聯絡喔!

類似用法

☞ Don't forget to keep in touch.
不要忘記要保持聯絡!

☞ Keep in touch with each other, OK?
要彼此保持聯絡，好嗎?

基本用語

Track 171

Call me sometime.

有空要打電話給我。

深入分析

sometime是指未來的某個時間點，表示希望彼此能透過互通電話，以保持聯絡的意思。

應用會話

A: Call me sometime.
有空要打電話給我。

B: I will.
我會的。

A: See you around.
再見囉！

B: Call me sometime.
有空要打電話給我。

類似用法

☞ Give me a ring sometime.
有空打電話給我。

☞ Give me a call if you have a chance.
有機會的話打電話給我。

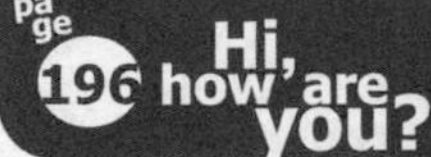

基本用語

Track 172

Calm down.

冷靜一下!

深入分析

當對方在生氣、暴怒或失去理智的情況下,你可以勸對方冷靜不要生氣的意思。

應用會話

A: I'm so angry about it.
我對這件事很生氣。

B: Calm down, pal. Don't lose your cool.
夥伴,冷靜一下!別失去理智。

A: I can't believe it. She left me at all.
我不敢相信,她終究離開我了!

B: Calm down.
冷靜一下!

類似用法

☞ Cool down.
冷靜一下!

☞ Keep your cool.
冷靜點!

基本用語

Track 173

Take it easy.

放輕鬆點!

深入分析

勸對方要放鬆心情、冷靜下來，有輕鬆面對、處理的意思。

應用會話

A: What happened to Mark? It's pretty late now.
馬克發生了什麼事? 現在很晚了。

B: Take it easy. He'll be all right.
放輕鬆點!他沒事的。

A: Don't you think it's unfair to me?
你不覺得對我是不公平的嗎?

B: Take it easy.
放輕鬆點!

類似用法

☞ Easy!
放輕鬆!

☞ Just relax.
放鬆一下!

基本用語

Track 174

Don't worry.

不要擔心！

深入分析

要對方放心、不要這麼憂心忡忡的意思，可以是對人或對事物的放心之意。

應用會話

A: My God! You scared me!
我的天啊！你嚇到我了。

B: Don't worry.
不要擔心！

A: Don't worry. It was only an accident.
不要擔心！這只是意外。

B: Are you sure about it?
你確定？

A: It's awful.
真糟糕。

B: Don't worry.
不要擔心。

基本用語

Track 175

Don't worry about me.

不要擔心我。

深入分析

可能是對方明顯表達對你的憂心，你就可以明確告知對方自己很好、不必為自己掛心、擔心的意思。

應用會話

A: Are you all right?
你還好嗎?

B: Don't worry about me.
不要擔心我。

A: You look so upset.
你看起來好沮喪!

B: Don't worry about me.
不要擔心我。

A: Sorry, I can't stay.
抱歉，我得走了!

B: Don't worry about me.
不要擔心我。

基本用語

Track 176

I'm so worried about you.

我真的很擔心你。

深入分析

表示自己很擔心對方的身心等各種狀況，總之就是放不下心的意思。

應用會話

A: I'm so worried about you.
我真的很擔心你。

B: Don't worry about me. It's nothing.
別擔心我，沒事。

A: I'm so worried about you.
我真的很擔心你。

B: I'm fine.
我很好啊！

基本用語

Track 177

Cheer up.

高興點！

深入分析

鼓勵對方、不要再這麼喪志，並要用開朗的心態來面對問題。

應用會話

A: Hey, cheer up!
嘿！高興點！

B: How could you say that?
你怎麼能這麼說？

A: Cheer up!
高興點！

B: I just can't.
我辦不到！

A: I trust you. Don't worry about it.
我相信你！不要擔心。

B: Thank you for cheering me up.
謝謝你鼓勵我。

基本用語

Track 178

What are friends for?

朋友就是要互相幫助！

深入分析

通常是朋友有難，而你願意提供協助，但對方可能會拒絕，你仍堅持要幫助時的用語。

應用會話

A: I don't know how to thank you.
我真不知道該如何感謝你。

B: Oh, come on. What are friends for?
喔！拜託。朋友就是要互相幫助！

A: What are friends for?
朋友就是要互相幫助！

B: It's so sweet to hear that.
真是貼心啊！

基本用語

Track 179

You deserve it.

你應得的!

深入分析

當對方面對長久以來的壓抑、不受重視後，如今撥雲見日時，你再次錦上添花力挺的意思。

應用會話

A: I got that promotion.
我終於升遷了。

B: You deserve it.
你是應得的!

A: So good? I don't believe it.
有這麼好? 我才不相信。

B: Oh, come on. You deserve it.
喔! 別這樣! 是你應得的!

基本用語

Track 180

Can I get you alone?

我能不能跟你單獨相處一會兒?

深入分析

get you alone字面意思是「獨自得到你」，其實就是「私底下獨處，並聊一聊」的意思。

應用會話

A: Can I get you alone?
我能不能跟你單獨相處一會兒?

B: Sure. What is the matter with you?
可以啊!你怎麼啦?

A: Can I get you alone?
我能不能跟你單獨相處一會兒?

B: Of course. What's up?
好啊!什麼事?

類似用法

☞ Can I speak to you in private?
我可以私底下和你談一談嗎?

基本用語

Track 181

Can I talk to you?

我能和您談一談嗎?

深入分析

直接表示希望能和對方對談、聊一聊的意思，通常要聊的是較嚴肅的話題。

應用會話

A: Can I talk to you?
我能和您談一談嗎?

B: What's up?
什麼事?

A: It's about Jack.
是有關傑克的事!

A: Can I talk to you?
我能和您談一談嗎?

B: About what?
要談什麼?

A: Can I talk to you?
我能和您談一談嗎?

B: Not now, please.
拜託，現在不方便!

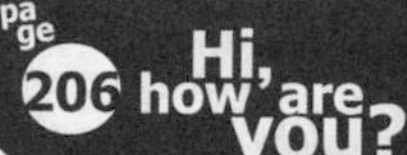

基本用語

Track 182

Got a minute to talk?

現在有空談一談嗎?

深入分析

表示希望和對方聊一聊(to talk)，而且不會佔用對方太多時間的意思，也可以只是問"Got a minute?"。

應用會話

A: Got a minute to talk, John?
約翰，有空談一談嗎?

B: Sure. Have a seat.
當然有! 坐吧!

A. Got a minute?
有沒有一點時間（談幾句話)?

B: Sorry, I'm quite busy now.
抱歉，我現在很忙。

類似用法

☞ Can I get you a second?
我可以佔用你一點時間嗎?

☞ Do you have a second now?
你現在有空嗎?

基本用語

Track 183

It won't keep you long.

不會耽誤你太久。

深入分析

表示自己接下來要做的事不會花太多的時間，也可以表示不會耽誤對方太多時間的意思。

應用會話

A: It won't keep you long.
不會耽誤你太久。

B: No problem. Have a seat.
沒問題啦!坐吧!

A: It won't keep you long.
不會耽誤你太久。

B: What can I do for you?
我能幫你做什麼?

類似用法

☞ It won't be long.
不會花太久的時間!

基本用語 Track 184

Let's change the subject.

我們換個話題吧!

深入分析

表示你不願意再繼續目前彼此正在聊的這個話題，是暗示想要轉移話題的好方法。

應用會話

A: So you still love that guy, don't you?
所以你還是愛那傢伙對吧?

B: Let's change the subject.
我們換個話題吧!

A: Let's change the subject.
我們換個話題吧!

B: You don't want to talk about it?
你不想討論這件事?

基本用語

Track 185

I don't want to talk about it.

我不想討論這件事。

深入分析

直接說明自己不想討論正在談的話題，或不願意回應對方提出的話題。

應用會話

A: I don't want to talk about it.
我不想討論這件事。

B: Why not?
為什麼不想?

A: I don't want to talk about it.
我不想討論這件事。

B: Please? It won't be long.
拜託啦!不會花太久的時間!

類似用法

☞ Let's stop talking.
不要再說了!

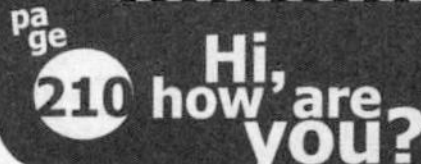

Track 186

Let's talk about it later.

晚一點再聊吧!

深入分析

可能表示自己目前沒有空討論，而非不想討論，建議晚一點或再找時間討論的意思。

應用會話

A: Let's talk about it later.
晚一點再聊吧!

B: Sure.
當然好。

A: Let's talk about it later.
晚一點再聊吧!

B: Why?
為什麼?

A: Something wrong?
有問題嗎?

B: Let's talk about it later.
晚一點再聊吧!

基本用語

Track 187

Congratulations!

恭喜!

深入分析

恭喜對方的常用語句,通常是發生好事或喜事時使用,不可以只說"Congratulation",一定要用複數形式的"Congratulations"。

應用會話

A: I got that promotion.
我升遷了。

B: Congratulations.
恭喜!

A: I'm going to be a dad.
我要當爸爸了!

B: Congratulations.
恭喜!

基本用語

Track 188

Could you give me a hand?

你能幫我一個忙嗎?

深入分析

give someone a hand字面意思雖是給某人一隻手，卻是「幫忙」的意思。

應用會話

A: Could you give me a hand?
你能幫我一個忙嗎?

B: Sure, what is it?
好啊，什麼事?

A: Could you give me a hand?
你能幫我一個忙嗎?

B: Sorry, not now.
抱歉，我現在沒有空!

類似用法

☞ Give me a hand!
幫幫我!

☞ Do me a favor.
幫我一個忙。

基本用語

Track 189

I need your help.

我需要你的協助。

深入分析

直接開口說明需要對方的協助的意思。

應用會話

A: Are you busy now?
你現在忙嗎?

B: No. What's up?
沒有! 什麼事?

A: I need your help.
我需要你的協助。

A: I need your help.
我需要你的協助。

B: Go ahead.
說吧!

基本用語

Track 190

Can you help me with this?

可以幫我這個忙嗎?

深入分析

help someone with something，表示需要幫某人做某事之意。

應用會話

A: Can you help me with this?
可以幫我這個忙嗎?

B: Of course.
當然好。

A: Can you help me with this?
可以幫我這個忙嗎?

B: I'm in the middle of something.
我(現在)手頭上有事。

A: Can you help her with it?
你可以幫她處理這件事嗎?

B: Me? No, I can't.
我? 不行，我辦不到!

基本用語

Track 191

May I help you?

需要我效勞嗎?

深入分析

主動詢問是否需要幫忙的用語，通常適用在正式場合。

應用會話

A: May I help you?
需要我效勞嗎?

B: Yes, please move it to the conference room.
是的，請把它搬到會議室。

類似用法

☞ Do you need any help?
你需要幫助嗎?

☞ What can I do for you?
我能為你做什麼?

☞ How can I help you?
我要怎麼幫你?

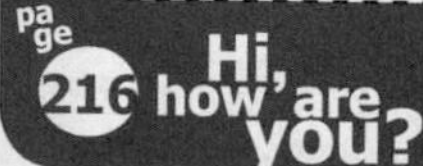

基本用語

Track 192

I'll see what I can do.

我來看看我能幫什麼忙！

深入分析

表示願意提供協助，但不是很確定是否能幫上什麼忙，是非常普遍使用於提供協助的前言。

應用會話

A: I'll see what I can do.
我來看看我能幫什麼忙！

B: You are so kind.
你真好心！

A: I'll see what I can do.
我來看看我能幫什麼忙！

B: It's good to have you here.
有你真好！

A: I'll see what I can do.
我來看看我能幫什麼忙！

B: Please don't bother.
不必麻煩了！

基本用語

Track 193

What makes you think so?

你為什麼會這麼認為?

深入分析

表示想要知道，造成對方形成目前這個想法的原因。

應用會話

A: Well, I don't think so.
嗯，我不這麼認為。

B: What makes you think so?
你為什麼會這麼認為?

A: What makes you think so?
你為什麼會這麼認為?

B: You tell me.
你說呢?

A: What makes you think so?
你為什麼會這麼認為?

B: Because of the car accident.
是因為那場車禍。

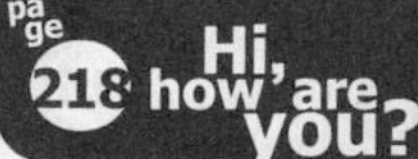

基本用語

Track 194

Did I make myself clear?

我說的夠清楚了嗎?

深入分析

make myself clear字面意思是讓我變得清楚，也就是想要知道對方是否懂你所要表達的意思。

應用會話

A: Did I make myself clear?
我說的夠清楚了嗎?

B: Yes, sir.
是的，老師。

A: Stop it. Did I make myself clear?
住手!我說的夠清楚了嗎?

B: I'll try my best.
我盡量。

A: Enough! Did I make myself clear?
夠了!我說的夠清楚了嗎?

B: It won't happen again.
不會有下一次了!

基本用語

Track 195

Is that clear?

夠清楚嗎?

深入分析

clear是清楚的，通常是指明白、瞭解、易懂的意思，表示詢問對方是否了解、清楚所有的事。

應用會話

A: Is that clear?
夠清楚嗎?

B: Very much.
非常清楚!

A: Is that clear?
夠清楚嗎?

B: I don't get it.
我不懂。

基本用語

Track 196

Do you hear me?

有聽懂我的意思了嗎?

深入分析

字面意思雖然是「你有聽見我嗎」，但其實是詢問對方有沒有聽懂你的說詞的意思。

應用會話

A: Do you hear me?
有聽懂我的意思了嗎?

B: Yes, I do.
是的，我懂!

A: Do you hear me?
有聽懂我的意思了嗎?

B: Yeah. Take it or leave it.
懂! 接受，不然就放棄。

類似用法

☞ Have you got it?
明白了嗎?

基本用語

Track 197

Don't make fun of me.

不要嘲笑我!

深入分析

fun是開心，make fun of someone則是嘲笑某人的意思。

應用會話

A: Don't make fun of me.
不要嘲笑我!

B: As you wish.
就依你!

A: Too bad.
太糟了!

B: Don't make fun of me.
不要嘲笑我!

類似用法

☞ Don't laugh at me.
別嘲笑我!

☞ Don't tease me.
別挖苦我!

☞ Get off my back!
不要嘲笑我!

基本用語

Track 198

You teased me.

你在嘲笑我。

深入分析

tease是言語上的嘲笑的意思，也有戲弄或逗弄的意思。

應用會話

A: You teased me.
你在嘲笑我。

B: It's because you are so funny.
因為你很有趣。

A: You teased me.
你在嘲笑我。

B: I didn't.
我沒有!

基本用語

Track 199

What are you laughing at?
你在笑什麼?

深入分析

laugh at是嘲笑的意思，嘲笑某人的常用片語就是laugh at someone。

應用會話

A: What are you laughing at?
你在笑什麼?

B: It's no big deal.
沒什麼大不了!

A: What are you laughing at?
你在笑什麼?

B: Forget it.
算了!

類似用法

☞ Stop laughing at me.
不要再笑我了!

基本用語

Track 200

Never mind.

算了！

深入分析

規勸或安慰對方不用在意、不用放在心上的意思，也適合在你欲言又止時的自我解嘲情境下使用。

應用會話

A: I was wondering...
我在懷疑…

B: Wondering what?
懷疑什麼？

A: Never mind. I don't want to know anymore.
算了，反正我也不想要知道了！

類似用法

☞ Forget it.
算了！

☞ It's nothing.
沒有什麼的！

☞ It's no big deal.
沒什麼大不了！

☞ It doesn't matter.
沒關係！

基本用語

Track 201

Don't even think about it.

想都別想！

深入分析

要對話方、死心、放棄、不用有過多其他想法，也是針對對方的提議，要對方不要再說了的意思。

應用會話

A: Shall I take a taxi?
我應該要搭計程車嗎?

B: Don't even think about it.
想都別想!

A: Why don't we try this way?
我們何不試著這樣做?

B: Don't even think about it.
想都別想!

基本用語

Track 202

That's all right.

沒關係！

深入分析

表示同意、無所謂、沒關係的意思。

應用會話

A: Thanks for coming.
謝謝你的來訪。

B: That's all right.
不客氣！

A: I can drive you home - it's really no bother.
我真的可以送你回家，不會麻煩的！

類似用法

☞ It's all right.
沒關係！

☞ It's OK.
沒關係！

☞ It doesn't matter.
沒關係！

基本用語

Track 203

No problem.

好，沒問題!

深入分析

字面意思是「沒問題」，但可以同時表示願意、答應、不成問題、沒關係、不必客氣的意思。

應用會話

A: Do you mind waiting for me?
你介意等我嗎?

B: No problem.
好，沒問題!

A: Would you do me a favor?
你可以幫我一個忙嗎?

B: No problem. What's up?
好，沒問題!是什麼事?

基本用語

Track 204

Don't take it so hard.

看開一點!

深入分析

表示不要嚴肅對待，也就是勸對方不要這麼想不開。

應用會話

A: I can't believe it.
我不敢相信!

B: Don't take it so hard.
不要把事情看得這麼嚴重。

A: What a letdown!
真令人失望!

B: Don't take it so hard.
看開一點!

類似用法

☞ Take it easy.
放輕鬆點!

基本用語

Track 205

Let it be.

就讓它過去吧!

深入分析

表示讓它成為過去，也就是對方正在困擾的事，心理上應該要放下，不要再困擾的意思。

應用會話

A: I can't believe it.
真教人不敢相信!

B: Let it be.
就讓它過去吧!

A: We aren't meant to be, are we?
我們不應是如此啊，不是嗎!

B: Just let it be.
就讓它過去吧!

基本用語

Track 206

Everything will be fine.

凡事都會沒問題的!

深入分析

表示目前的困難或困境,遲早都會解決,不必為此如此擔心的意思。

應用會話

A: You must be kidding.
你是在開玩笑的吧!

B: You know what? Everything will be fine.
你知道嗎? 凡事都會沒問題的!

A: Thank you for cheering me up.
謝謝你鼓勵我。

A: Everything will be fine.
凡事都會沒問題的!

B: I hope so.
希望是這樣!

基本用語

Track 207

I know how you feel.

我瞭解你的感受!

深入分析

表示針對對方目前所面臨的困境或窘境，你能夠感同身受，有站在同一陣線的意思。

應用會話

A: Is that a joke?
是開玩笑的嗎?

B: I know how you feel.
我瞭解你的感受!

A: I didn't mean that.
我不是那個意思。

B: I know how you feel.
我瞭解你的感受!

類似用法

☞ I know how you must feel.
我能理解你的感受。

基本用語

Track 208

Let me drive you home.

讓我載你回家。

深入分析

drive someone home表示開車送某人回家的意思。

應用會話

A: Don't worry. Let me drive you home.
不用擔心!讓我載你回家。

B: I'm sorry to bother you.
抱歉麻煩你了!

A: Let me drive you home.
讓我載你回家。

B: You have been very helpful.
你幫了很大的忙。

類似用法

☞ Want a lift?
要搭便車嗎?

基本用語

Track 209

Can you give me a lift?

可以開車送我一程嗎?

深入分析

要求對方給自己一程，也就是開車讓你搭便車到某地的意思，lift是指「搭便車」、「順路搭載」。

應用會話

A: Can you give me a lift?
可以開車送我一程嗎?

B: Sure. Let's go.
好啊!走吧!

A: Can you give me a lift?
可以開車送我一程嗎?

B: I don't think so.
沒辦法!

基本用語

Track 210

What's the rush?

趕著要去哪裡?

深入分析

可能是在路上偶遇某人，而對方看起來似乎在趕路，就可以問:"What's the rush?"，表示詢問急著去哪裡的意思。

應用會話

A: What's the rush?
趕著要去哪裡?

B: I have to be home before two o'clock.
我要在兩點鐘前回到家。

A: What's the rush?
趕著要去哪裡?

B: I'm going to meet my parents at the airport.
我要去機場接我父母的飛機。

基本用語

Track 211

I'm falling in love with him.

我愛上他了！

深入分析

fall in love就是中文的「陷入愛河」，也就是在戀愛中的意思。

應用會話

A: I'm crazy for David!
我為大衛瘋狂！

B: David? I can't believe it.
大衛？我真是不敢相信！

A: I'm falling in love with him.
我愛上他了！

A: Stop calling Eric!
不要再打電話給艾瑞克了。

B: But I'm falling in love with him.
但是我愛上他了。

基本用語

Track 212

I can't live without her.

沒有她我活不下去!

深入分析

表示無法在沒有對方的狀況下苟活的意思。若對方是男性則用"whithout him"。

應用會話

A: I can't live without her.
沒有她我活不下去!

B: Wake up.
別作夢了!

A: What happened?
發生什麼事了?

B: I can't live without her.
沒有她我活不下去!

A: He's not your Mr. Right.
他不是你的真命天子!

B: But I can't live without him.
但是沒有他我活不下去!

基本用語

Track 213

I just can't help it.

我就是情不自禁。

深入分析

help是幫助的意思，但也有情不自禁做某事的意思。

應用會話

A: My God! Why did you do that?
我的天啊！你為什麼這麼做？

B: I just can't help it.
我就是情不自禁。

A: You really made me feel embarrassed.
你讓我出糗了！

B: I just can't help it.
我就是情不自禁。

基本用語

Track 214

Give me a break.

饒了我吧!

深入分析

字面意思是給我一個休息，其實是要對方別鬧了、饒了我的意思，類似中文「你少來了」的用法。

應用會話

A: David is my big brother.
大衛是我大哥。

B: David? Come on, give me a break.
大衛? 得了吧，少來了!

A: You have to finish it on time.
你要如期完成這件事。

B: Oh, give me a break.
喔，饒了我吧!

基本用語

Track 215

Come on!

你少來了!

深入分析

當對方的某種言行讓你不認同時，就可以用玩笑、調侃的語氣要對方不要這麼做的意思。

應用會話

A: David is going to visit her parents.
大衛要去拜訪她的雙親。

B: Come on, I don't believe it.
少來了，我才不相信。

A: I've got so much to do.
我有一堆事情要做。

B: Come on!
你少來了!

基本用語

Track 216

Get out!

少來了！

深入分析

除了是要對方滾蛋，還有要對方不要開玩笑、嚴肅一點的意思。

應用會話

A: David called me last night.
大衛昨天晚上打電話給我了。

B: Get out!
少來了！

A: Why don't you try to do it?
你為什麼不試著做這件事？

B: Get out!
少來了！

基本用語

Track 217

I don't buy it.

我不相信!

深入分析

字面意思是「我不會買」，其實就是類似中文「我不會買帳」、「我不相信」的意思。

應用會話

A: I don't buy it.
我不相信!

B: We will see.
那就等著瞧吧!

A: Hurry up, or we'll be late.
快一點，不然我們要遲到了。

B: I don't buy it.
我不相信!

類似用法

☞ I don't believe it.
我才不相信。

基本用語

Track 218

What does it meant?

那是什麼意思?

深入分析

表示對某件事、某標誌、意象或某人的言行不瞭解的意思。

應用會話

A: What does that mean?
這是什麼意思?

B: You tell me!
你說呢?

A: It's worth a shot.
那值得一試。

B: What does it mean?
那是什麼意思?

A: You'll never know what you can do until you try.
你不試試看永遠不會知道!

基本用語

Track 219

What do you mean by that?

你這是什麼意思?

深入分析

表示不清楚對方的意圖，by that是特指對方所說或所做的那一件事。

應用會話

A: Tell me the secret between you guys.
告訴我你們之間的秘密。

B: What do you mean by that?
你這是什麼意思?

A: What do you mean by that?
你這是什麼意思?

B: I'm not telling.
我不會回答你的問題。

A: Come on, this is yours.
好了，這是你的了!

B: What do you mean by that?
你這是什麼意思?

基本用語

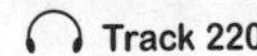

It's not what I meant.

那不是我的意思。

深入分析

表示對方的解讀已經造成誤會，或因此誤會你，是你對自己的言行捍衛、辯解的意思。

應用會話

A: I'm tired of helping him.
我對於要幫助他這件事感到厭煩了。

B: You can't be serious.
你不是當真的吧?

A: It's not what I meant.
那不是我的意思。

A: It's not what I meant.
那不是我的意思。

B: Are you sure?
你確定嗎?

類似用法

☞ I didn't mean that.
我不是那個意思。

基本用語

Track 221

I didn't mean to.

我不是故意的。

深入分析

表示自己不是故意做某事的意思，通常是無意中冒犯了對方的情境下使用。to後面可以接動詞，表示不是故意做某事的意思。

應用會話

A: You stepped on me.
你踩到我了！

B: Sorry, I didn't mean to.
抱歉，我不是故意的。

A: I didn't mean to.
我不是故意的。

B: It's OK.
沒關係！

A: I didn't mean to hurt you.
我不是故意要傷害你。

B: Say no more.
不要再説了！

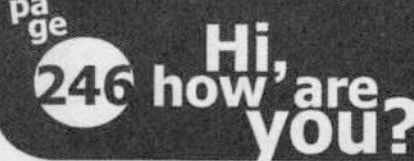

基本用語

Track 222

I don't want this.

我也不想要這樣！

深入分析

表示面對目前發生的狀況，自己也感到很無奈，不願意面對這樣的發展結果的意思。

應用會話

A: I thought you should be in the office right now.
我以為你現在應該在辦公室。

B: I don't want this.
我也不想要這樣！

A: I bet you'll have to pay for it.
我敢說你一定會為此事付出代價。

B: I don't want this.
我也不想要這樣！

基本用語

Track 223

Says who?

誰說的?

深入分析

表示當你聽聞某一事件時，感到不相信、不可思議，想要知道這些事是由誰傳出來的。

應用會話

A: Now what?
現在該怎麼辦?

B: We'll find the answer eventually.
最終我們會找到答案的。

A: Says who?
誰說的?

A: Says who?
誰說的?

B: David.
是大衛說的!

基本用語

Track 224

Hurry up!

快一點！

深入分析

催促對方加緊速度，不要拖拖拉拉的意思。

應用會話

A: Hurry up, or we'll be late.
快一點，不然我們要遲到了。

B: It's still early.
還很早啊！

A: Hurry up! It's ten-thirty now.
快一點！現在十點卅分了！

B: I'm not ready yet.
我還沒準備好！

類似用法

☞ Hurry!
快一點！

基本用語

🎧 Track 225

Cool.

真酷!

深入分析

cool字面意思是「冷的」，和中文口語常用的「酷」的意思一樣，都有覺得很炫、很棒的意思。

應用會話

A: Look!
看!

B: Cool. Where did you get this?
真酷! 哪來的?

A: How do you like it?
你覺得怎麼樣?

B: Cool.
真酷喔!

類似用法

☞ It's so cool.
真酷!

☞ It's awesome.
真酷!

基本用語

Track 226

That's really something.

那真是了不起!

深入分析

字面意思是「真的有一些事」，但其實something表示具有某些特點的人事物，所以衍生為了不起的意思。

應用會話

A: That's really something.
那真是了不起!

B: I think so too.
我也是這麼認為。

A: That's really something.
那真是了不起!

B: Are you sure?
你確定嗎?

A: Yeah! Why not?
是啊! 怎麼不是?

基本用語

Track 227

We have a deal.

我們已經有共識了!

深入分析

deal是交易的意思，have a deal是表示彼此已經達成共識，或「我們就這樣說定了」的意思。

應用會話

A: We have a deal.
我們已經有共識了!

B: We do?
我們有嗎?

A: Are you sure about it?
你確定嗎?

B: Yeah! We have a deal.
是啊!我們已經有共識了!

A: It's too good to be true.
哪有這麼好的事!

類似用法

☞ Deal.
就這麼說定了!

基本用語

228

It's no big deal.

沒什麼大不了！

深入分析

字面意思是「不是大的交易」，衍生為不用太大驚小怪的意思。

應用會話

A: It's no big deal.
這沒什麼大不了啊！

B: Hey, don't ever say that again.
嘿，不要再這麼說了！

A: You didn't do it on time
你沒有準時完成喔！

B: It's no big deal.
這沒什麼大不了啊！

類似用法

☞ No big deal.
沒什麼大不了！

基本用語

Track 229

I'm counting on you.

萬事拜託了！

深入分析

count on someone表示依賴某人的意思，也就是拜託某人做某事的意思。

應用會話

A: I'm counting on you.
萬事拜託了！

B: No problem.
沒問題的啦！

A: I quit.
我不幹了！

B: You can't. I'm counting on you.
你不能這樣啦！我很依賴你啊！

類似用法

☞ I count on you.
我很依賴你。

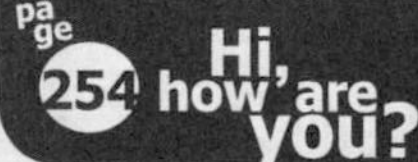

基本用語

Track 230

We will see.

再說吧！

深入分析

字面意思雖然是「我們會看見」，但其實是指現在無法做出決定，要等之後的情況再來決定的意思。

應用會話

A: Can I go to her home and stay the night?
我可以去她家過夜嗎?

B: We will see.
再說吧!

A: Maybe he's my Mr. Right.
也許他是我的真命天子。

B: We will see.
我們等著瞧吧!

類似用法

☞ I will see.
再說吧!

基本用語

Track 231

It depends.

看情況再說!

深入分析

表示事件的發展還無法確定，會因為其他因素受到影響，所以要看情況再來討論的意思。

應用會話

A: What are you going to do?
你打算怎麼作?

B: I have no idea. It depends on the situation.
我不知道。要視情況而定。

類似用法

☞ It depends.
視情況而定。

☞ Could be, but I'm not so sure.
有可能，但是我不確定。

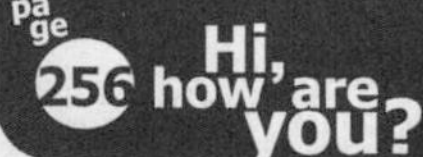

基本用語

Track 232

It's enough.

夠了!

深入分析

表示「這一切都夠了!」,是指面對現在的狀況感到有點無奈,希望到此為止的意思。

應用會話

A: He bit me.
他咬我。

B: But he bit me too.
但是他也有咬我。

C: It's enough. I'll punish both of you.
夠了,我兩個人都要處罰!

A: It's enough. It's pretty dangerous.
夠了!很危險的。

B: I don't think so.
我不這麼認為!

類似用法

☞ Enough.
夠了!

基本用語

Track 233

Stop it.

住手!

深入分析

表示對於目前遭受到的待遇或狀況感到極度的厭惡、不滿...等，希望對方不要再做或說某事的意思。

應用會話

A: Stop it.
住手!

B: Sure. As you wish.
好啊!就如你所願!

A: Stop it.
住手!

B: Why?
為什麼?

A: Don't do this anymore.
不要再這麼做了!

A: Stop it, guys.
各位，住手!

B: None of your business.
少管閒事!

基本用語

Track 234

Excuse me.

借過一下。

深入分析

Excuse me.可以表示「借過」、「抱歉」、「打擾」的意思，若是後面兩種意思，通常你還會有後面接下來要做或說的事。

應用會話

A: Excuse me.
借過。

B: Sure.
好啊!

A: Will you excuse us?
請容我們先離席好嗎?

B: Go ahead.
去吧!

A: Excuse me.
請問一下?

B: Yeah?
有什麼事?

A: Where am I now?
這裡是哪裡?

基本用語

Track 235

I didn't do anything.

我什麼事也沒做。

深入分析

表示自己並沒有任何作為，通常適用在對方誤會你做了某事時使用。

應用會話

A: Don't move.
別動！

B: I didn't do anything.
我什麼事也沒做。

A: May I see your ID?
我可以看你的身份證嗎？

B: Sure. I didn't do anything.
好啊！我什麼事也沒做。

類似用法

☞ I did nothing.
我什麼事也沒做。

基本用語

Track 236

Stay where you are.

待在原地!

深入分析

喝阻對方的用語，表示要對方待在原地不要亂動的意思，通常是警察對嫌疑犯的威嚇用語。

應用會話

A: Stay where you are.
待在原地!

B: What happened?
發生什麼事了?

A: Stay where you are.
待在原地!

B: All right.
好!

類似用法

☞ Don't move.
別動!

☞ Freeze!
別動!

基本用語

Track 237

Hands up!

手舉起來!

深入分析

當警方面對現行犯時，一定會要對方手舉起來，一方面要對方乖乖束手就擒，也能看清對方手上是否有武器。

應用會話

A: Hands up!
手舉起來!

B: What's going on?
發生了什麼事?

A: Hands up!
手舉起來!

B: I did nothing wrong.
我沒做錯事啊!

基本用語

Track 238

It's a good idea.

好主意!

深入分析

讚賞對方提出的好方法或好建議的意思。

應用會話

A: Why don't we try this restaurant?
為什麼我們不試試這間餐廳?

B: It's a good idea.
那是一個好主意!

A: How about a cup of coffee?
要不要喝杯咖啡?

B: It's a good idea.
那是一個好主意!

類似用法

☞ That's a great idea!
好主意!

☞ Sounds good.
聽起來不錯!

基本用語

Track 239

How much is it?

這個要多少錢?

深入分析

詢問對方某物的售價是多少錢的意思。

應用會話

A: How much is it?
這個要多少錢?

B: It's one hundred dollars.
這個要一百元。

A: How much is it?
這個要多少錢?

B: It's not for sale.
這個東西是非賣品。

類似用法

☞ How much does it cost?
這個賣多少錢?

☞ How much did you say?
你說要多少錢?

基本用語

Track 240

I'll take it.

我決定要買了。

深入分析

字面意思是「我要拿它」，其實是決定要買某個商品時，告訴店員自己要買的意思，類似中文「幫我打包起來」的意思。

應用會話

A: How do you like it?
你喜歡嗎?

B: It looks great. I'll take it.
看起來不錯耶! 我決定要買了。

類似用法

☞ I'll take this one.
我要買這一個。

☞ I'll buy this one.
我要買這一個。

基本用語

Track 241

It happens.

常有的事。

深入分析

表示現在的狀況是見怪不怪，對方不用這麼訝異，有找理由規避責任的意味。

應用會話

A: He is so weird. What is he doing out there?
他好奇怪。他在那裡做什麼?

B: It happens.
常有的事。

A: It's ridiculous, right?
真的很荒謬，對嗎?

B: It happens.
常有的事。

類似用法

☞ It happens all the time.
常有的事!

☞ It's no big deal.
這沒什麼大不了!

基本用語

Track 242

It's going to happen.

事情百分百確定了。

深入分析

字面意思是將會再發生，也就是事情百分百確定了，有點無力可回天的無奈意思。

應用會話

A: I don't think it's a good idea.
我覺得這不是一個好主意。

B: I know, but it's going to happen.
我知道，但事情已經百分百確定了。

A: It's going to happen.
事情百分百確定了。

B: Yeah! What can we say?
是啊!我們還能說什麼?

基本用語

Track 243

How come?

為什麼?

深入分析

字面意思是「如何來」，但how come其實是表示詢問原因的意思。

應用會話

A: I missed the train this morning.
我今天早上錯過火車了。

B: How come?
為什麼?

A: I really hate her.
我真的很討厭她。

B: How come?
為什麼?

類似用法

☞ Why?
為什麼?

☞ What for?
為什麼?

基本用語

Track 244

Why not?

為什麼不要?

深入分析

當對方提出某個否定的觀念、想法或建議時，你就可以持反面的問句質疑對方，也可以當成答應、同意的用語。

應用會話

A: I don't want this one.
我不想要這個!

B: Why not?
為什麼不要?

A: I don't like to go out with them.
我不喜歡和他們一起出去。

B: Why not?
為什麼不喜歡?

A: Do you want to join us?
要加入我們嗎?

B: Why not?
好啊!

基本用語

Track 245

I'm glad to hear that.

我很高興知道這件事。

深入分析

當你聽到對方提起某件事，你因此感到高興或開心，就可以說"glad to hear that"。

應用會話

A: We are going to study in L.A.
我們就要去洛杉磯唸書了。

B: I'm glad to hear that.
我很高興知道這件事。

A: They decided to get married next month.
他們打算下個月結婚。

B: I'm glad to hear that.
我很高興知道這件事。

類似用法

☞ I'm happy to hear that.
我很高興聽見這件事。

基本用語

Track 246

I'm really happy for you.

我真為你感到高興。

深入分析

表示自己真心替對方感到開心的意思，通常是對方發生好事的情境時使用。

應用會話

A: I decided to quit.
我決定辭職了。

B: I'm really happy for you.
我真為你感到高興。

A: I had a good time.
我玩得很開心。

B: I'm really happy for you.
我真為你感到高興。

基本用語

Track 247

Good for you.

對你來說是好事。

深入分析

對方的某件事對他自己是好的，就可以直接說明，也用於讚賞對方的決定或行為是對的。

應用會話

A: I have to stop drinking.
我得要戒酒!

B: Good for you.
對你來說是好事。

A: I have to take the medicine.
我得要吃藥。

B: Good for you.
對你來說是好事。

基本用語

Track 248

I'm not telling.

我不會說。

深入分析

表示守口如瓶，自己不會輕易說出任何話或洩密的意思。

應用會話

A: Tell me your secret.
告訴我你的秘密。

B: I'm not telling.
我才不會説。

A: I'm not telling.
我不會説。

B: You can't be serious.
你不是當真的吧?

類似用法

☞ I'm not going to tell you.
我不打算告訴你。

☞ I won't let you know.
我不會讓你知道!

基本用語

Track 249

No comment.

不予置評!

深入分析

字面意思是「不評論」，也就是不願意說出任何事實或評論的意思。

應用會話

A: What do you think of it?
你覺得這個如何?

B: No comment.
不予置評!

A: Come on!
你少來了!

B: No comment.
不予置評!

A: Anything you say.
隨便你怎麼說都可以!

基本用語

Track 250

I'm not myself today.

我今天什麼都不對勁！

深入分析

表示今天的我不同於以往的我，也就是不順利的意思。

應用會話

A: You look terrible. What's wrong?
你看起來糟透了！怎麼啦？

B: I don't know. I'm not myself today.
我不知道，我今天什麼都不對勁！

A: Are you all right?
還好吧？

B: I'm not myself today.
我今天什麼都不對勁！

類似用法

☞ I was having a bad day.
我今天做什麼事都不太對勁。

基本用語

Track 251

I don't know.

我不知道。

深入分析

表示自己一無所知、不瞭解、不確定...等的意思。

應用會話

A: Do you know where the park is?
你知道公園在哪裡嗎?

B: Sorry, I don't know.
抱歉，我不知道!

A: Don't you want this?
你不想這樣嗎?

B: Well... I don't know.
嗯，我不知道。

類似用法

☞ I have no idea.
我不知道。

☞ I have no clue.
我不知道。

基本用語

Track 252

I don't know for sure.

我不太清楚。

深入分析

表示自己不但不知道，更無法確認某些事的意思。

應用會話

A: Where am I on this map?
我在這張地圖上的哪裡?

B: I don't know for sure.
我不太清楚。

A: Where are you trying to go?
你想要去哪裡?

B: I don't know for sure.
我不太清楚。

類似用法

☞ I don't really know.
我不太清楚。

基本用語

Track 253

I don't know for sure at the moment.

我現在還不知道!

深入分析

表示到目前為止(at the moment)，仍舊不知道或不確認的意思。

應用會話

A: What happened to David?
大衛發生什麼事了?

B: I don't know for sure at the moment.
我現在還不知道!

A: How is she now?
她現在如何?

B: I don't know for sure at the moment.
我現在還不知道!

基本用語

Track 254

I know nothing about it.

我一無所知!

深入分析

表示自己所知的是nothing，也就是完全不知道的意思。

應用會話

A: What a mess over here.
這裡真是一團亂!

B: Don't look at me. I know nothing about it.
不要看我!我一無所知!

C: It's my fault, mom.
媽咪，是我的錯!

類似用法

☞ I don't know what you are talking about.
我不知道你在說什麼。

☞ I don't know, either.
我也不知道!

基本用語

Track 255

You're not listening to me.

你沒在聽我說！

深入分析

質疑對方沒有仔細聽自己的言論。也帶有對方不聽話、不遵從你的建議的意思。

應用會話

A: Do I make myself clear?
我說的夠清楚了嗎？

B: I... you know...
我...你知道的...

A: You're not listening to me.
你沒在聽我說！

A: You're not listening to me.
你沒在聽我說！

B: Sorry, I didn't mean to.
抱歉，我不是故意的。

基本用語

Track 256

I can't believe it.

我真不敢相信！

深入分析

可能是發生令人訝異的事，表示令人不敢相信的意思。

應用會話

A: I can't believe it.
我真不敢相信！

B: It's OK!
沒關係！

A: David and Jane broke up last week.
大衛和珍上週分手了。

B: I can't believe it.
我真不敢相信！

A: Check it out.
你看！

B: Oh, I can't believe it.
喔！我真不敢相信。

基本用語

Track 257

It's impossible.

不可能！

深入分析

表示所發生的事應該是不可能，也表示發生的機率很低的意思。

應用會話

A: It's impossible.
不可能！

B: I have no other choice.
我別無選擇。

A: It's impossible.
不可能！

B: Why not?
為什麼不可能?

類似用法

☞ It's absolutely impossible.
這是絕對不可能的！

☞ It can't be.
不可能的事！

基本用語

Track 258

Is that so?

真有那麼回事嗎?

深入分析

表示懷疑事件的真實性，帶有不敢相信的意味。

應用會話

A: I got stuck at the airport.
我被困在機場了。

B: Is that so?
真有那麼回事嗎?

A: I missed the train.
我錯過火車了。

B: Is that so? Liar.
是嗎? 你說謊。

類似用法

☞ Really?
真的?

☞ Is that true?
真是事實嗎?

基本用語

Track 259

I have a question.

我有一個問題!

深入分析

表示自己有問題想要提出來討論或得到對方解釋、說明的意思。

應用會話

A: I have a question.
我有一個問題!

B: Go ahead.
你說吧!

A: Is that a problem?
有問題嗎?

B: Yes, I have a question.
是的，我有一個問題!

A: Something wrong?
有問題嗎?

B: Yes, I have a question.
是的，我有一個問題!

基本用語

Track 260

No shit!

不會吧!

深入分析

字面意思是沒有排泄物，也就是發生不可思議的事時，自己不敢相信的隨口回應語。

應用會話

A: No shit! Why did you do that?
不會吧!你為什麼這麼做?

B: I have to.
我必須這麼做!

A: No shit!
不會吧!

B: It's up to you. You are the boss.
由你決定!你說了就算!

基本用語

Track 261

I agree with you.

我同意你。

深入分析

agree with someone表示同意某人已發表的觀點或想法。

應用會話

A: This plan is still up in the air.
這個計畫仍舊懸而未決。

B: I agree with you.
我同意你。

A: I agree with you.
我同意你。

B: Good. I'm looking forward to it.
很好!我很期待!

類似用法

☞ I couldn't agree more.
我完全同意。

基本用語

Track 262

I couldn't agree less.

我是絕對不會同意的。

深入分析

表示同意無法再少了，也就是你保持堅決反對立場的意思。

應用會話

A: I think it's a great opportunity.
我認為這是一個好機會。

B: I don't think so. I couldn't agree less.
我不這麼認為。我是絕對不會同意的。

類似用法

☞ I don't agree with you.
我不同意你的意見。

☞ I don't agree on that.
我不同意這件事。

基本用語

Track 263

I don't have time.

我沒有空。

深入分析

沒有空就是沒有時間，time就是空閒的意思。

應用會話

A: You really need to take a break.
你真的需要休息一 下!

B: I don't have time.
我沒有空。

A: Can you walk my dog after dinner?
晚餐後你可以幫我遛狗嗎?

B: I don't have time.
我沒有空。

類似用法

☞ I have no time.
我沒有時間。

☞ I don't have time to do it.
我沒有時間去做。

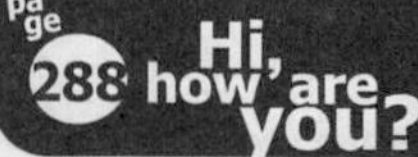

基本用語

Track 264

I'm quite busy now.

我現在很忙。

深入分析

busy是忙碌的，非常忙碌就是quite busy的意思。

應用會話

A: Busy now?
現在在忙嗎?

B: Yeah, I'm quite busy now.
是啊，我現在很忙。

A: Would you do me a favor?
可以幫我一個忙嗎?

B: I'm quite busy now.
我現在很忙。

類似用法

☞ I'm very busy right now.
我現在很忙。

☞ I'm in the middle of something.
我現在手頭上有事。

基本用語

Track 265

I'm afraid not.

恐怕不行喔!

深入分析

通常是拒絕或反對對方的意思，表示自己的否定沒那麼確認的含蓄用語，也帶有「不好意思這麼做」的意味。

應用會話

A: Can you help me?
你能幫我嗎?

B: I'm afraid not.
恐怕不行喔!

A: Can you talk for a minute?
有空聊一聊嗎?

B: I'm afraid not.
恐怕不行喔!

A: How about this?
這個怎麼樣?

B: I'm afraid not.
恐怕不行喔!

基本用語

Track 266

I guess I will.

也許我會。

深入分析

當對方提出某個建議或未來是否會...的問題，若你的回答是肯定會，就可以直接說："I guess I will."，加了 I guess...表示應該是這樣的意思。

應用會話

A: Why don't you call her again? You still love her.
你何不再打電話給她?你依然愛著她啊!

B: I guess I will.
也許我會（打電話給她）。

A: I guess I will.
也許我會。

B: Good for you.
對你來說是好事!

基本用語

Track 267

I guess so.

我想是吧!

深入分析

認為目前的狀況是如此，這個狀況(so)是彼此都知道的狀況。

應用會話

A: It's a lot of hard work.
這工作很不簡單。

B: I guess so.
我想是吧!

A: Look, can you keep a secret?
聽好，你能保守秘密嗎?

B: I guess so.
我想是吧!

基本用語

Track 268

Maybe, maybe not.

可能吧!

深入分析

針對現在的狀況，會有兩種正反不同的結果，自己也不確定的意思。

應用會話

A: Can you tell the difference between them?
你可以分辨他們兩者之間的不同嗎?

B: Maybe, maybe not.
可能吧!

A: Any other colors?
有沒有其他顏色?

B: Maybe, maybe not.
可能吧!

A: What do you mean by that?
你是什麼意思?

類似用法

☞ Yes and no.
也是也不是!

基本用語

Track 269

I have no choice.

我別無選擇。

深入分析

表示自己實在是沒有其他選擇才會這麼做，有點無奈的意味。

應用會話

A: Why did you do that?
你為什麼這麼做?

B: I have no choice.
我別無選擇。

A: I have no choice.
我別無選擇。

B: Oh, dear. I'm sorry to hear that.
哎呀!這太遺憾了!

類似用法

☞ I have no options.
我別無選擇。

☞ I have no other choice.
我別無選擇。

☞ There is no choice.
別無選擇。

基本用語

Track 270

It's up to you.
由你決定。

深入分析

口語化用法，表示決定權在對方手上，也有隨便對方怎麼做的意思。

應用會話

A: I don't want to talk about it.
我不想討論這件事。

B: It's up to you.
由你決定!

A: It's up to you.
由你決定!

B: No. You are the boss.
才不呢!你說了就算!

類似用法

☞ Up to you.
由你決定。

基本用語

Track 271

You decide.

由你決定!

深入分析

通常不是說明語句,而是代表催促對方趕快下決定的意思。

應用會話

A: What's the writing topic?
寫作的主題是什麼?

B: You decide.
由你決定!

A: You decide.
由你決定!

B: Me? I don't think so.
我? 不要吧!

基本用語

Track 272

Make up your mind.

作個決定吧!

深入分析

勸對方趕緊做出決定，mind表示想法，make up someone's mind表示要某人做出決定的意思。

應用會話

A: Maybe I should go to see a doctor.
也許我應該去看醫生。

B: Make up your mind.
作個決定吧!

A: I like the style, but not the color.
我喜歡這個款式，但是不喜歡這個顏色。

B: Make up your mind.
作個決定吧!

類似用法

☞ It's your own decision.
這是你自己要做的決定。

基本用語

Track 273

I have decided.

我已經決定了!

深入分析

利用完成式語(have decided)表示自己已經下了某個決定,希望對方不要再勸自己改變主意的意思。

應用會話

A: I have decided.
我已經決定了!

B: Good.
很好!

A: I have decided.
我已經決定了!

B: So? Show us.
所以呢? 秀給我們看!

基本用語

Track 274

I haven't decided yet.

我還沒有決定。

深入分析

表示自己尚未決定，句尾加了yet表示「尚未...」，所以對方可能還有機會改變你的想法，或是請對方再給自己多一點的時間。

應用會話

A: Are you ready to order?
你要點餐了嗎?

B: I haven't decided yet.
我還沒有決定。

A: I haven't decided yet.
我還沒有決定。

B: No problem.
沒關係!

基本用語

Track 275

I hope so.

希望如此。

深入分析

雖然是對於對方的言論不置可否，也可以是真心期望如此的意思，有時也帶有看笑話的意味。

應用會話

A: You can do your best to finish it.
你可以盡你所能去完成。

B: I hope so.
我也希望是如此。

類似用法

☞ I hope you are right.
希望你是對的！

☞ I guess so.
我猜也是如此。

☞ I think so.
我想也是如此。

☞ That's what I expect.
那就是我所期望的！

基本用語

Track 276

I warned you.

我警告過你了。

深入分析

表示自己以前曾經提醒過對方，但對方可能置之不理，後來真的發生這件事時，就可以這麼回應對方，通常表示不好的事件。

應用會話

A: My God! It's so terrible.
我的天啊！真是糟糕！

B: I warned you.
我警告過你了。

A: I warned you yesterday.
我昨天就警告過你了。

B: I didn't expect it to happen.
我沒有預期會發生這件事。

類似用法

☞ I told you so.
我已經告訴過你(會發生這個情形)了。

基本用語

Track 277

I've told you not to do it.

我告訴過你不要這麼做了!

深入分析

表示自己以前曾經告誡過對方不要做某事，但有可能對方不理會仍舊如此作為，卻發生不好的事時，你的再次提醒用語。

應用會話

A: I've told you not to do it.
我告訴過你不要這麼做了!

B: Sorry for that.
我為那件事抱歉啦!

A: Shit!
慘了!

B: I've told you not to do it.
我告訴過你不要這麼做了!

基本用語

Track 278

I'll do my best.

我會盡力的!

深入分析

表示自己會盡力做某事，要對方不要擔心自己的意思。

應用會話

A: Can you finish it on time?
你可以準時完成嗎?

B: I'll do my best.
我盡量。

A: I'll do my best.
我會盡力的!

B: Wonderful! That's good for you.
太好了。那對你很好。

類似用法

☞ I'll try my best.
我盡量。

基本用語

Track 279

Try again.

你再試試。

深入分析

鼓勵對方再試一次、不要輕言放棄的意思。

應用會話

A: Try again.
你再試試。

B: I don't think so.
我辦不到!

A: Try again.
你再試試。

B: Sure. I'll try again.
好! 我會再試一次!

基本用語

Track 280

I'll try.

我會試試看。

深入分析

表示曾經失敗過，而自己願意再試一次，希望對方再給自己一次機會的意思。

應用會話

A: I'll try.
我會試試看。

B: Thank you so much.
非常感謝!

A: Why don't you ask him for help?
你為什麼不向他求助?

B: I'll try it.
我會試試看。

類似用法

☞ I'll take a shot.
我會試試。

☞ I'll try again.
我會再試一次!

基本用語

Track 281

I'll say.

的確是這樣。

深入分析

字面意思雖然是「我會說」，但其實是某人發表某種言論後，得到你的肯定的意思。

應用會話

A: I don't think it's her fault.
我不覺得是她的錯。

B: I'll say.
的確是這樣的。

A: I'll say.
的確是這樣。

B: I don't get it.
我不懂。

基本用語

Track 282

In or out?

你到底要不要參加?

深入分析

詢問對方是否要參加某個大家說好了要一起參與的活動，表示定要參加(in)或退出(out)的問句。

應用會話

A: In or out?
你到底要不要參加?

B: OK, I'll go with you.
好，我會和你一起去。

A: In or out?
你到底要不要參加?

B: I'm in.
我要參加。

類似用法

☞ Coming or not?
到底要不要來?

基本用語

Track 283

Count me in.

把我算進去。

深入分析

當大家邀約著要一起參加某個活動時，在一旁的你也願意加入這個活動，就可以說："Count me in."，表示算我一份加入的意思。

應用會話

A: Anyone else?
還有人(要去)嗎?

B: Count me in.
把我算進去。

A: Are you in or out?
你到底要不要參加?

B: Count me in.
把我算進去。

基本用語

Track 284

I quit.

我退出。

深入分析

可以是「我辭職」、「我不幹」，或是放棄原本正在從事的活動或是計畫，表示退出這一切的意思。

應用會話

A: Who is with me?
有誰要一起參加?

B: I quit.
我退出。

A: I quit.
我退出。

B: Anyone else?
還有人（要退出）嗎?

基本用語

Track 285

It's getting worse.

事情越來越糟了。

深入分析

表示目前事情的狀況，已經比彼此原先知道還要嚴重許多的意思。

應用會話

A: How's it been going?
近來如何?

B: It's getting worse.
事情越來越糟了。

A: It's getting worse.
事情越來越糟了。

B: Oh, I'm sorry to hear that.
喔，真是遺憾!

類似用法

☞ Worse, I guess.
我想很糟吧!

基本用語

Track 286

It's about time.

時候到了。

深入分析

不是「大約時間」的意思，而是暗喻「時候到了，該做某事」，但沒有說明要做哪件事，因為彼此心知肚明的意思。

應用會話

A: It's about time.
時候到了。

B: Time for what?
是時候要做什麼?

A: Time to go to school.
該去上學了!

A: It's about time.
時候到了。

B: Yeah! Time to work it out.
是啊!該解決了!

基本用語

Track 287

Time to go.

該走了!

深入分析

全文為"It's time to go."，表示該是到了要離開的時候，也就是你準備要道別的意思。

應用會話

A: Shall we?
可以走了嗎?

B: Yeah! Time to go.
是啊!該走了!

A: Time to go.
該走了!

B: I'm not ready yet.
我還沒準備好。

A: Time to go.
該走了!

B: I don't think so.
我不這麼認為。

基本用語

Track 288

It's a long story.

說來話長。

深入分析

long story是指很長的故事，也就是「說來話長」的意思，表示要說的事情相當冗長，以確認對方是否願意聽的意思。

應用會話

A: We broke up last month.
我們上個月分手了。

B: How come?
為什麼?

A: It's a long story.
說來話長。

A: It's a long story.
說來話長。

B: Try me.
說來聽聽!

基本用語

Track 289

It's a piece of cake.

太容易了。

深入分析

字面意思是指一片蛋糕，也就是非常簡單的意思，表示對方提出的幫忙要求，自己是願意、也可以處理，甚至是小事一樁的意思。

應用會話

A: Show me how to do it.
示範給我看要怎麼做。

B: A piece of cake!
這太簡單了!

A: What would you do with it?
你會怎麼做?

B: It's a piece of cake.
太容易了。

基本用語

Track 290

No sweat.

沒問題！

深入分析

字面意思是沒有流汗，也就是沒問題、包在我身上的意思，表示答應對方的請求、願意幫忙的意思。

應用會話

A: Can you help me with this?
可以幫我這個忙嗎？

B: No sweat.
沒問題！

A: Do you need any help?
你需要幫助嗎？

B: Yeah. See that?
是啊！有看到嗎？

A: No sweat.
沒問題！

基本用語

Track 291

It's my fault.

這都是我的錯。

深入分析

將一切的責任歸屬攬在自己身上，帶有表示願意承擔錯誤的意味。

應用會話

A: I was wondering why it happened.
我懷疑這件事為什麼會發生。

B: It's my fault.
這都是我的錯。

A: Who did this?
誰幹的好事?

B: It's my fault.
這都是我的錯。

類似用法

☞ My bad.
是我的錯。

基本用語

Track 292

I made a mistake.

我弄錯了！

深入分析

承認自己犯了一個錯誤的意思，雖然沒有道歉的語句，但其實就是承認錯誤的意思。

應用會話

A: What a mess over here.
這裡真是一團亂！

B: Sorry, I made a mistake.
抱歉，我弄錯了！

A: I made a mistake.
我弄錯了！

B: It's OK.
沒關係！

基本用語

Track 293

It'll all work out.

事情會有辦法解決的。

深入分析

work out除了是健身，還有解決的意思，加了all有強調全部的事的意思，通常是要對方不必擔心所有不好的事。

應用會話

A: I'm sorry to hear that.
我很遺憾聽見這件事!

B: It'll all work out.
事情會有辦法解決的。

A: It'll all work out.
事情會有辦法解決的。

B: I hope so.
希望如此。

基本用語

Track 294

So what?

那又怎樣?

深入分析

反問對方那又如何，表示無奈、不認同，也有你能奈我如何的意思。

應用會話

A: I can expect it.
我想也是!

B: So what?
那又怎樣?

A: David and I went to see a movie.
我和大衛有去看過電影。

B: So what? I don't care at all.
那又怎樣? 我一點都不在意。

基本用語

Track 295

I don't care at all.

我一點都不在意。

深入分析

表示對於自己的行為有信心，不在意他人的想法的直接用語，at all表示完完全全的意思。

應用會話

A: It's going to be over soon.
事情很快就會過去的。

B: So? I don't care at all.
那又如何? 我一點都不在意。

A: You didn't tell your parents?
你沒有告訴你的父母?

B: Nope. I don't care at all.
沒啊!我一點都不在意。

類似用法

☞ I don't care.
我不在意。

基本用語

Track 296

Who cares!

誰在乎啊！

深入分析

字面意思是誰在乎?表示包括自己在內，沒有任何人會在意的意思，有憤世嫉俗的意味。

應用會話

A: I think he is so mean.
我覺得他真是惡毒。

B: So what? Who cares!
那又怎樣? 誰在乎!

A: I'm telling the truth.
我說的是事實!

B: Who cares!
誰在乎啊!

基本用語

Track 297

Nobody cares!

沒有人會在乎!

深入分析

沒有人會在乎，表示不受到重視，這句話有點無奈、淒涼的意味。

應用會話

A: What kept you so late?
什麼事讓你耽擱得這麼晚?

B: Nobody cares!
沒有人會在乎!

A: Come on, I do.
不要這樣!我在意啊!

A: Something wrong?
有事嗎?

B: Nobody cares!
沒有人會在乎!

基本用語

Track 298

It means nothing.

沒啥意義!

深入分析

nothing表示沒有事，也就是沒有意義、不重要的意思。

應用會話

A: What happened between you guys?
你們之間發生了什麼事?

B: Forget it. It means nothing.
算了! 沒啥意義!

A: It means nothing.
沒啥意義!

B: What are you trying to say?
你想要説什麼?

基本用語

Track 299

It's none of your business!

你少管閒事!

深入分析

字面意思為「不是你的事業」，也就是表示希望對方不要插手、不要管閒事的意思。

應用會話

A: Don't let the failure get you down.
不要讓這次的失敗使你沮喪。

B: It's none of your business!
你少管閒事!

A: There you are.
你又來了!

B: It's none of your business!
你少管閒事!

類似用法

☞ None of your business!
你少管閒事!

基本用語

Track 300

It's not the point.

這不是重點。

深入分析

表示現在討論的不是重點，重點似乎被忽略了，希望能重新正視問題。

應用會話

A: I don't give a shit what David thinks.
我才不管大衛的想法!

B: It's not the point.
這不是重點。

A: Are you saying not to complete it?
你是說不要去完成嗎?

B: You are wrong. It's not the point.
你錯了!那不是重點。

A: It's over between us, Chris.
我們之間完了，克里斯!

B: It's not the point.
那不是重點。

基本用語

Track 301

Anyone else?

還有其他人要嗎?

深入分析

通常是詢問在場的第三方，針對之前問過的相同問題，詢問第三方的答案的意思。

應用會話

A: May I have another new one?
可以再給我另一個新的嗎?

B: Sure. Anyone else?
好的。還有其他人(要)嗎?

A: Anyone else?
還有其他人(要)嗎?

B: No, thanks.
不用了，謝謝!

類似用法

☞ Anything else?
還有其他事嗎?

☞ Something else?
還有要其他東西嗎?

基本用語

Track 302

Is that all?

全部就這樣嗎?

深入分析

通常是對方下結論或拿某物給你時，你想要確定「是否這些就是全部」的意思。

應用會話

A: Check this out.
你看!

B: Is that all?
全部就這樣嗎?

A: Here you are.
給你。

B: Is that all?
全部就這樣嗎?

A: I don't think so.
我不這麼認為!

基本用語

Track 303

Watch this.

看我的!

深入分析

當你要對方看你的表現或作為時，中文可以說「看我的」，轉換為英文該怎麼說呢?可不是"Watch me"，而是"Watch this"。當然這句話也可以是表示叫對方注意看的意思。

應用會話

A: Watch this.
看我的!

B: Wow! It's so incredible.
哇!真是不可思議啊!

A: Isn't it too difficult to you?
對你來説不會太難嗎?

B: Not at all. Watch this.
一點都不會!看我的!

基本用語

Track 304

Aren't you gonna do something?

你不想點辦法嗎?

深入分析

當事情陷入困境，而你希望督促對方能想辦法解決時，就可以說"Aren't you gonna do something?"也就是中文「你不想點辦法來解決嗎?」的意思。

應用會話

A: Aren't you gonna do something?
你不想點辦法嗎?

B: What am I supposed to do?
我能怎麼辦?

A: Aren't you gonna do something?
你不想點辦法嗎?

B: No, I am not.
不，我不打算要!

類似用法

☞ Do something.
你得想辦法解決。

基本用語

Track 305

Never.

從沒有過！

深入分析

除了可以回答「從未...」的意思，也可以在對方提議並詢問你的意見時，回答"Never."表示「從來不列入考慮」的意思。

應用會話

A: Have you ever been to Hong Kong?
你去過香港嗎？

B: Never.
從沒有去過！

A: How about this one?
這個如何？

B: Never.
想都別想！

基本用語

Track 306

I bet.

我敢打賭!

深入分析

表示對自己或對方的言論感到肯定、絕對是如此，類似中文「要不要打賭就是這樣」的意思。

應用會話

A: I don't think you could make it. I bet.
我不這麼認為你辦得到!我敢打賭。

B: Why not?
為什麼辦不到?

A: He'll have to pay for it.
他一定會為此事付出代價。

B: I bet.
我敢打賭（是這樣的）!

基本用語

Track 307

When are you leaving for L.A.?

你什麼時候要啟程去洛杉磯?

深入分析

"leave for + 地點"是指「出發啟程到某地點」的意思。

應用會話

A: When are you leaving for L.A.?
你什麼時候要啟程去洛杉磯?

B: This Friday.
這個星期五。

A: When are you leaving for L.A.?
你什麼時候要啟程去洛杉磯?

B: Well... I've got to think about it.
嗯，我要想一想。

基本用語

Track 308

Anytime.

隨時都歡迎！

深入分析

通常是對方感謝你的付出、幫助時，你回應對方「不客氣」的意思，表示「我隨時都很歡迎你提出要求協助」。

應用會話

A: Thank you for your help.
謝謝你的幫助！

B: Anytime.
隨時都歡迎！

A: So sorry to bother you.
很抱歉打擾你。

B: Anytime.
隨時都歡迎！

基本用語

Track 309

Sorry, I took so long.

抱歉，耽擱這麼久!

深入分析

對於自己做某事的時間過長，以致於可能產生耽誤的行為感到抱歉的意思。

應用會話

A: Sorry, I took so long.
抱歉，耽擱這麼久!

B: I trust you. Don't worry about it.
我相信你，不要擔心。

A: Sorry, I took so long.
抱歉，耽擱這麼久!

B: Something wrong?
有什麼問題嗎?

基本用語

Track 310

I'll miss you.

我會想念你的!

深入分析

通常是即將要分別的人之間的用語，表示不捨得分開的意思。

應用會話

A: Call me sometime.
有空打個電話給我。

B: I'll miss you.
我會想念你的!

A: I'll miss you.
我會想念你的!

B: Me, too.
我也是。

基本用語

Track 311

What for?

為什麼?

深入分析

可以解釋為「為什麼」，通常是想要知道這有什麼意義或原因的意思。

應用會話

A: We really want to change the project.
我們真的很想改變計畫。

B: What for?
為什麼?

A: You will come, won't you?
你會過來，對吧?

B: What for?
為什麼?

基本用語

Track 312

How could I forget!

我怎麼會忘了呢?

深入分析

表示自己絕對、也不可能會忘記某些彼此正在討論的事，意指自己記性很好的意思。

應用會話

A: Don't you remember me?
你不記得我了嗎?

B: How could I forget!
我怎麼會忘了呢?

A: Aren't you Kenny?
你不是肯尼嗎?

B: How could you forget!
你怎麼會忘了呢?

基本用語

Track 313

That's fine with me.

我沒意見。

深入分析

通常是對方提出建議或想法時，你沒有意見甚至是同意的意思。

應用會話

A: How about having some coffee?
要不要喝點咖啡?

B: That's fine with me.
我沒意見。

A: I think I'd like to go to Greece.
我覺得我想要去希臘。

B: Greece, eh? Sure, that's fine with me.
希臘?嗯，我沒意見。

基本用語

Track 314

Good job.

幹得好！

深入分析

稱讚對方的好表現時，就可以說"Good job."，是非常常用的讚美語句。

應用會話

A: I've already finished it on time.
我已經如期完成了。

B: Good job.
幹得好！

A: I've found the solution.
我已經找到解決的方法了。

B: Good job.
幹得好！

類似用法

☞ Well done.
幹得好。

☞ Nice going.
幹得好。

☞ You did a great job.
你做得很好。

基本用語

Track 315

Not on your life.

一輩子都別想！

深入分析

表示要對方死心或放棄某一個想法或計畫，表示有自己在，對方別想要這麼做的意思。

應用會話

A: Can I have a dog?
我可以養狗嗎？

B: Not on your life.
一輩子都別想！

A: I really want to see her.
我真的很想和她見面。

B: Not on your life.
一輩子都別想！

基本用語

Track 316

I'd rather you didn't.

你最好是不要!

深入分析

通常是對方提出要求或請求時，若你的回答是屬於間接否定的情境，就可以說"I'd rather you didn't."。

應用會話

A: Do you mind if I smoke?
我可以抽菸嗎?

B: I'd rather you didn't.
你最好是不要!

A: May I?
我可以這樣嗎?

B: I'd rather you didn't do it.
你最好是不要這麼做!

基本用語

Track 317

Are you still upset?

你還在難過嗎?

深入分析

upset是指「沮喪的」，表示要知道對方是否心情還是不好或低落的意思。

應用會話

A: Are you still upset?
你還在難過嗎?

B: Kind of.
還有一點（難過）。

A: Are you still upset?
你還在難過嗎?

B: Me? Not at all.
我?沒有啊!

基本用語

Track 318

Take your time.

慢慢來不要急。

深入分析

安撫對方不用急、慢慢來，通常是指時間還很多，可以放心慢慢處理的意思。

應用會話

A: Out of my way. I am going to be late.
滾開，我快遲到了！

B: Take your time.
慢慢來，不要急！

A: Take your time.
慢慢來，不要急！

B: But time is up.
可是時間到了！

基本用語

Track 319

Something happened.

事情不太對勁喔!

深入分析

表示發現事情有蹊蹺，卻又不知是哪些問題，所以用something統稱所有的事，也可以解釋為「有事情發生」的意思。

應用會話

A: Something happened.
事情不太對勁喔!

B: Nothing is wrong with me.
我沒事啊!

A: Anything?
有什麼發現嗎?

B: Something happened.
事情不太對勁喔!

類似用法

☞ There must be something.
事情不太對!

基本用語

Track 320

Keeping busy?

在忙嗎?

深入分析

詢問對方現在是否正在忙，不是要對方忙，而是有事要打擾或討論之前的詢問語，以確定對方是否有空的意思。

應用會話

A: Keeping busy?
在忙嗎?

B: No, not at all. What's up?
不，一點都不會。有什麼事嗎?

A: Keeping busy?
在忙嗎?

B: A little bit.
有一點!

類似用法

☞ Are you busy now?
你現在在忙嗎?

基本用語

Track 321

Let's get it straight.

我們坦白說吧!

深入分析

表示希望兩人之間能開誠布公,彼此不要再有所隱瞞,直接將心裡的話說出來的意思。

應用會話

A: I think we should...
我覺得我們應該...

B: Let's get it straight.
我們坦白說吧!

A: Let's get it straight.
我們坦白說吧!

B: What are you trying to say?
你想要說什麼?

基本用語

Track 322

Any discount?

有沒有折扣?

深入分析

表示想要知道對方是否願意降價求售的意思，通常是暗示對方自己要議價的常用語。

應用會話

A: It's one thousand dollars.
這件要一千元。

B: Any discount?
有沒有折扣?

A: Any discount?
有沒有折扣?

B: I am afraid not.
恐怕沒有喔!

類似用法

☞ No discount?
沒有折扣嗎?

國家圖書館出版品預行編目資料

Hi! How are you 你一定要會的基本問候語 / 張瑜凌編著.
-- 初版. -- 新北市 : 雅典文化, 民102.09
面 ; 公分. -- (全民學英文 ; 33)
ISBN 978-986-6282-94-2(平裝附光碟片)
1.英語 2.會話
805.188 102013767

全民學英文系列 33

Hi! How are you 你一定要會的基本問候語

編　　著/張瑜凌
責　　編/張瑜凌
美術編輯/林于婷
封面設計/劉逸芹

法律顧問:方圓法律事務所/涂成樞律師

總經銷:永續圖書有限公司
永續圖書線上購物網
www.foreverbooks.com.tw

CVS代理/美璟文化有限公司
TEL:(02)2723-9968
FAX:(02)2723-9668

出版日/2013年09月

雅典文化

出版社
22103 新北市汐止區大同路三段194號9樓之1
TEL (02)8647-3663
FAX (02)8647-3660

全民學英文
33

Hi! How are you 你一定要會的基本問候語

雅致風靡　典藏文化

親愛的顧客您好，感謝您購買這本書。即日起，填寫讀者回函卡寄回至本公司，我們每月將抽出一百名回函讀者，寄出精美禮物並享有生日當月購書優惠！想知道更多更即時的消息，歡迎加入"永續圖書粉絲團"您也可以選擇傳真、掃描或用本公司準備的免郵回函寄回，謝謝。

傳真電話：（02）8647-3660　　電子信箱：yungjiuh@ms45.hinet.net

姓名：　　性別：　□男　□女

出生日期：　年　月　日　電話：

學歷：　　職業：

E-mail：

地址：□□□

從何處購買此書：　　購買金額：　元

購買本書動機：□封面 □書名 □排版 □內容 □作者 □偶然衝動

你對本書的意見：
內容：□滿意□尚可□待改進　編輯：□滿意□尚可□待改進
封面：□滿意□尚可□待改進　定價：□滿意□尚可□待改進

其他建議：

剪下後傳真、掃描或寄回至「22103新北市汐止區大同路3段194號9樓之1雅典文化收」

總經銷：永續圖書有限公司

永續圖書線上購物網

www.foreverbooks.com.tw

您可以使用以下方式將回函寄回。

您的回覆，是我們進步的最大動力，謝謝。

① 使用本公司準備的免郵回函寄回。

② 傳真電話：（02）8647-3660

③ 掃描圖檔寄到電子信箱：

yungjiuh@ms45.hinet.net

沿此線對折後寄回，謝謝。

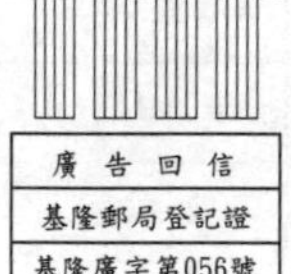

雅典文化事業有限公司　收

新北市汐止區大同路三段194號9樓之1

雅致風靡　典藏文化

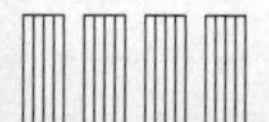